THE

SEQUEL

to

JANE AUSTEN'S

"PRIDE and PREJUDICE"

✣

"TRUST and TRIUMPH"

By

NORMA GATJE-SMITH

This book is a work of fiction. Places, events, and situations in this story are purely fictional. Any resemblance to actual persons, living or dead, is coincidental.

First published by AuthorHouse 08/04/04

ISBN: 1-4184-5887-2 (e-book)
ISBN: 1-4184-2659-8 (Dust Jacket)

Library of Congress Control Number: 2004105016

Printed in the United States of America
Bloomington, Indiana

This book is printed on acid free paper.

Biography

Norma Gatje-Smith grew up in New York City and graduated from the Art School of Pratt Institute.

She worked as a textile designer in the Netherlands and Manhattan until she moved to St. Joseph, Michigan, where she lives with her husband, Norman Smith, a former pilot.

Collages designed with calico fabric are her invention, and she has created many pictures, in this medium, of Victorian houses and country scenes.

Writing is her favorite pastime and she has written numerous articles for decorating magazines and humorous essays for "The Chicago Tribune".

At the end of "Pride and Prejudice", by Jane Austen, Mrs. Benet, known for her frantic matchmaking, relaxed in happiness as her daughters married the rich and aristocratic, Mr. Darcy and Mr. Bingley.

At that moment, the lives of all the characters exploded into dramatic and humorous adventures. There would no longer be Balls alone to provide diversion, there was romance and travel ahead for fun and excitement.

After a honeymoon of games and merriment, the Darcys return to Pemberley and discover there is a need for diligence to find suitable suitors for their sisters.

On their way to success, they encounter gypsy schemes and rescue pirates on their voyage to Savannah.

Jane has left their lives in my hands and I sensed her approval as I wrote.

Be prepared for mischief and romance!

For the overleaf of the book jacket.

Table of Contents

Chapter One

Trust and Triumph

A dazzling view of a hill covered with daffodils and lillies and a Heavenly duet coming from the music room, created a warmth to fill Fitz William Darcy's chest and center upon his heart as he gazed from his window on a remarkable spring morning.

He was a tall man of uncommonly fine features and aristocratic bearing and, as sometimes happens, was one of the handsome people who are unaware of the effect they have on their friends and passersby. The memory of one of his smiles lived in the happiest thoughts of women he had met or had merely passed in the village and his touch and handshake were felt over and over in their quiet and reflective moments. Watching him walk with his long legged stride and the graceful movement of his shoulders, to and fro, was a delight to make a woman feel joyful all the day.

Darcy's lack of conceit was, of all his characteristics, the strongest and most touching, yet he felt that his looks and wealth were nothing compared to his marriage to Elizabeth Bennet who bestowed on him his greatest honor when she became his wife.

He was amused on that morning as he pictured Elizabeth sliding easily out on satin sheets without disturbing him and he was excited by the mysterious concert as he pulled on his robe to go out and investigate. His five dogs always arranged themselves around his door at night, protecting them from whatever dog-imagined harm might be out in the corridor. They encircled him, jumpimg and dancing, so eager to begin the day as he patted them and led the way to the music room, William noted that Rumpus, a Corgi, with the most mischievous attitude and the head of a German Shepherd on the body of a Dachshund, had been shut in his sister's parlor. He was an affectionate animal who did his best to join anything resembling a social occasion at Pemberley. For this before dawn concert, he was in temporary seclusion because he loved to sit beside anyone singing or playing the piano, plunging right into the melodies with rending moans and brief staccato woofs.

William walked carefully on slippered feet, turned the corner slowly and soundlessly, and before the musicians sensed his presence, he joined Elizabeth in her song, one of his favorites, and that was the reason for the practise at dawn.

"We can not keep surprises and secrets from you!" exclaimed Elizabeth, as she rushed to him with a scolding finger, then a hug. "It is only seven and you need more sleep," she teased. "Here, take Rumpus, and the two of you can snuggle back to sleep."

"Elizabeth, my adorable darling, I have not pursued you all over Southern England and married you in a church to be told to snuggle in bed with a pup."

His sister, Georgianna, the pianist, joined the merriment. "There are certain things a husband must adjust to, William, we women have our eccentricities, some sleep til noon and others play the piano and sing before dawn. I have an idea, I will find Mrs. Reynolds and ask her to warm some bisquits and tea for us, then we can have a proper repast as I play some Bach for a breakfast serenade."

The two young ladies made the loveliest of pictures with lace night dresses and bright aureoles of their hair falling gently around their shoulders. Elizabeth's dark eyes and rosey pink complexion took her into the highest realms of perfect brunette English beauty and, in contrast, Georgianna with her golden curls and violet blue eyes, had the attitude and looks of an angel. When Elizabeth was angry she had an intense fiery expression, when Georgianna was angry, she still looked like an angel.

While trying to make William disappear, they exhibited a bit of each look and were so unknowingly seductive, he thought he had better take a walk outside with the dogs, and treating them to an indulgent smile, he left them to their music.

Fitz William Darcy was about ten years older than Georgianna and she had been left in his charge when their father died. He was devoted to her and it was his wish to be both brotherly and fatherly, by turns, and when she was at school in London, he felt he could finally relax.

William and Elizabeth Darcy were newlyweds and their marriage was like a love story. They cherished moments of

2

tenderness as they passed each other in their huge manor, busy with their daily activities. William gave her hugs and kisses and Elizabeth shared his endearments as they whispered about a baby Darcy, their dearest wish.

When she returned from errands in the village or finished practising, Georgie would ask where they were and Mrs. Reynolds acted truly baffled and answered, "You know, Miss Darcy, this is such an enormous house I can simply not keep track of them and it is vexing sometimes when a messenger comes to the door and wants Mr. Darcy to sign as he receives a letter. I send them down to the stables, where they are now well acquainted, while I shout up and down the halls and climb three stories looking for them and sometimes it gets so late, I serve tea to the messenger and later, supper. I must tell you though, it is a comfort to me to see the Master with smiles ready to break into grins of happiness. He was so sad and in the doldrums after your father died."

Georgianna knew they were in the manor because their carriage drivers were resting in the stables. She often wished for some neices and nephews rushing about and playing in Pemberley and she suddenly realized, with a thrill, they were in bed! She was an unsophisticated young woman and these sudden insights took her breath away. She too had noticed her brother's contented manner since he and Elizabeth married.

In the years the two of them were floundering without their parents, he acted stern with her and she would lie down and weep away from his sight. He was, after all, only in his twenties, but people seemed to expect more of him than his cold shyness and some times, ready scowls. Elizabeth was helping him with that. She was a warm and vivacious woman and she teased him relentlessly to make him laugh and hug her.

She had not done this since she was seven, but she was laughing so hard she skipped to the pond where she loved to sort out her deepest thoughts. "What a pair!", she thought. "Pemberley could burn down and they would go on with their love making under the covers. I think I will tease them and suggest they hang a bell with a loud gong downstairs so Mrs. Reynolds can find them in a hurry for the messengers."

3

In the years before he met Elizabeth, William would see beautiful women and desire them but he drew himself up short as he noticed traits that Georgie would not like, and he felt he must find a companionable sister-in-law for her almost to the exclusion of his own needs. He wrestled in his mind with scruples and sadly began to think of Georgianna as another big chore when she was really a sweet and lovely child who needed a mother. He often thought of her as a child and did not sense that she had adult thoughts and attitudes. Georgianna would humor him because she knew he was trying so hard but sometimes she had to restrain herself when he smoothed out the ringlets on her forehead, dabbed little stains off her coat, scolded when she forgot to practise and read to her at night to entertain her. She liked Shakespeare and Romance novels.

He allowed her to buy one novel every other week and read through them to cancel out risqué passages she might find before he could censor them. His idea of a piece he should censor was "Gregory put Hellena's coat lovingly around her shoulders." "What could he possibly do to find out if she knew the facts of life? One day he had a sudden brainstorm.

Mrs. Reynolds, his housekeeper, whom he regarded almost as a grandmother, would be the perfect person to tell her! She agreed completely and reminded William that she had always thought of the Darcys as her grandchildren.

William said he wanted her to start with stories of the baby animals, specifically about one of their horses who had birthed a foal the past week.

She walked with Georgie to sit on a bench by the pond and not one to procrastinate or mince words, she said directly, that when adults were in love and married, they undressed and lay down together. Then they pressed close beneath their waists and…"Oh, this is daunting…well, perhaps it would be best if you go to the barn and look under the animals to see how they differ…a goat would be good, not a horse, he might kick you. And, be sure to do it early in the morning so the servants do not see you."

Georgie giggled, "Mrs. Reynolds, I sense the fine hand of my brother in this. The girls in school talk of almost nothing else but the

Birds and the Bees and I know all about where babies come from, I do not have to look under a goat!"

The housekeeper squeezed her hand and hurried up to the manor to ready lunch, with relief and some amusement.

....

With all his anxiety and confusion about finding the perfect woman to marry, William was beginning to dread marriage as a business arrangement and for him, that would be insufferable.

The predicament of his and Georgie's future gave him an every day pain in the head.

To distract himself, he swam, dueled, hunted, and studied until his great friend, Charles Bingley, invited him to a ball in the countryside. He insisted that he go along to swell the ranks of male dancers and Darcy was feeling self conscious and put upon.

"Do you have to lean against the wall wearing that sulky, superior expression? For God's sake, Darcy, can you not find one beauty to ask to dance?" Bingley had an almost perpetual enthusiastic attitude and, at the moment, he was enchanted with Jane Bennet, a sweet blonde, whom everyone considered the most beautiful young woman in town. "She only wants his money. I know the look. I have seen it often enough," Darcy thought.

Suddenly, a dark haired dancer, whispered something in Jane's ear and they looked at him with smiles. He caught that. At first glance, she was a vision of all he considered lovely in a woman- dark flirting eyes, graceful movements and a most becoming blush that crept across her face as she caught his eye again. The reason for the whispering must have been for Jane to tell her that he had a fortune.

He stormed out of the ballroom and searched for a cool balcony. He looked at a star and a song he remembered from childhood teased him as he laughed and said "Star light, star bright, first star I see tonight, I wish I may, I wish I might, have the wish I wish tonight." He laughed again to himself, and noticed a pleasant surge of warmth. His head had stopped aching.

5

He felt like kneeling but just leaned against a balustrade and prayed, "Dear Lord, forget my prayers for Georgianna temporarily, I must have that woman."

The mothers who sat around the edge of the ballroom had been studying this new man with intense interest. It was close to the end of the Napoleonic wars and so many Englishmen of marriageable age had died fighting for the future lives of their families, there were few eligible men walking or dancing in England and searching for wives.

Darcy stopped at the door of the balcony long enough to see the dark beauty laughing and talking with friends and he thought, "Stupid man, why can I not simply walk up to her and ask for the next dance?"

He waited a few minutes until he saw Bingley and then went to be introduced to Jane.

"Darcy, you are right on time, go over and ask Jane's sister, Elizabeth, for a dance. She is the dark haired one who has been watching you all evening." Jane smiled as if to urge him on.

"Oh no, I have something on my mind."

And with that, he nearly ran to the balcony to be alone. And safe.

Darcy thought it was almost as if Elizabeth sought him out and he knew, through gossip, that her mother was the pushiest and most matrimonially minded matriarch in town.

Elizabeth was ordered by her mother to introduce herself but she felt timid when she approached and found him with his arms tightly crossed and wearing an unpleasant frown.

The other observant mothers, who wished for almost nothing more than husbands for their daughters, whispered among themselves that even though he was rumored to have great wealth and a manor the size of the Queen's palace, they must discourage him.

This Fitz William Darcy acted like a superior aristocrat, the worst sort to consider as a future son-in-law.

The balls continued at a frantic pace, two a week and not a single proposal. Mrs. Bennet observed that the young soldiers who came to the balls must be shell shocked from the war as none of them were seeking out her daughters to marry. All the girls and their

6

mothers thought the soldiers, who were stationed in Meryton, looked eminently marriageable, but in truth, they were biding their time waiting for girls with large dowries.

In the ensuing week, Darcy rode to London to ask Georgianna to help him brush up on his dancing while they caught up on news and laughed and planned together. She suspected that he had fallen in love, really smitten, and she had never seen him so joyful and merry, keeping his secret. She taught him some new steps, learned at Miss Underwood's Academy of the Dance, to embellish his style, and it was so delightful, William felt serene and confident, better than he had in his teens.

Georgianna hugged him over and over and told him he was the sweetest brother, never realizing she was the only woman fortunate enough to embrace him.

The next ball was considered an important one, a sort of masquerade with dancers wearing eye masks. William had no trouble finding a masked Elizabeth, He thought about how she looked every minute of every day. He walked up to her and signed for two dances on her nearly filled dance card, hoping his terrible nervousness would leave him in time. He prayed to feel very calm. The mothers were out in full force warning their daughters that they did not want Mr. Darcy for a son-in-law even though the girls thought he was devinely handsome and wished the mothers would relent, if only for a short waltz. This very attractive, well educated, and wealthy man was in their midst wanting to be accepted and all they could feel was apprehension.

The dances went badly for William. Elizabeth had heard all the warnings and she was unsmiling and cold during the Quadrille.

Fitz William Darcy was a man of passion and did nothing methodically. He felt an ardent unremitting desire for Elizabeth and was thrown off balance. He arrived, uninvited, in Bennet's parlor one day and proposed marriage in the most awkward way, pointing out that her family was uneducated and middle class and not even close to his aristocratic standards. Of course, she became almost insanely angry and Elizabeth Bennet was not one to ever mince words. She told him that if he owned all the palaces in England, Scotland, and

Wales, she would not marry him and she would not marry him, as well, if he were the proverbial last man on Earth.

She hurt him terribly, but her courage and spirit in handling him, made him desire her even more.

When Elizabeth visited her dearest friend, Charlotte, a newly married minister's wife, she learned that William's aunt lived nearby. The Fates seemed to be guiding him handsomely to pursue Elizabeth and he turned up with a regularity she could not understand. She liked determined people, but she wished he would move far, far away. On a walk downtown, she glimpsed him from the side of her eye as he approached with a letter and begged her to read it. He stated his innocence in some matters the town gossips circulated about him, and as she read it, she was humiliated to remember her harsh answer to his proposal.

The problem with Darcy was that she did not want him to go entirely away. She loved to look at him and know that he desired her. Before she fell asleep at night, she could think of nothing but his beautiful face and body and wonder what it would be like if he caressed her and put his hands lightly on her back to press close.

He had quite a scar on his side forehead. He must have been in danger. Whenever she saw him, she wanted to kiss it.

What a shame it was that his personality was strange and complex, but that was what made him so fascinating.

As she sat in church with Charlotte one Sunday, she was provoked with him again as he walked boldly into their pew and sat beside her. She frowned at his greeting and moved closer to her friend, refusing to sing with his hymnal as he offered to share it, and stood coldly with her arms crossed. She would never know that he had planned this encounter carefully, sat hidden in his carriage until he saw them enter, and then waited a few minutes til they were seated. He had come in hopes that he could smell her flowery perfume and listen to her sing the hymns because he thought her voice was the loveliest he had heard. Charlotte gave her a nudge- she knew what was happening in this little drama beside her.

"What a beautiful singing voice he had." She had admired his fine speaking voice. "Why, oh, why, was she not allowed to forget him?" She had not been this close to him, ever, and now she took in

8

his natural scent, just like pines and fresh air. "He must walk his dogs in the forest," she thought. His hands were large with long tapering fingers and his narrow feet were encased in expensive riding boots. She felt like a colorless little country wren sitting beside him and she wished she had worn her lavender silk dress with the ecru lace. He was wonderfully charismatic and it pleased her to be so close to him, she could take in all his pleasant details in quick darting glances.

He sat loosely with his hands clasped in his lap and there was such a manliness radiating from him, she stood up suddenly, wanting to flee and started to sway towards him and bumped his elbow. "If only I could have this precious woman sitting beside me in church and on my arm as my wife.", he thought, wistfully and sadly." (There was no mind reading happening that morning.)

Elizabeth thought "Oh, Heavenly Father, I love this man and I should not! Please let the service be over soon!" She was so upset, she pushed her way out of the pew past him and she could not be sure, but it felt as if he patted her waist. "How dare he touch me? Oh, dear God, I hope he did, it felt so very exciting." In one second, she was going to fall in love with him!

She wondered if he still loved her. How could he? She told him that she just about despised him. His looks were perfect but she knew he was arrogant and thought her family was terribly middle class. "Oh, what a ghastly confusion! I think I would have wonderful looking sons if he were their father."

She was walking slowly, touching each pew to keep her balance. She loved sitting beside him but today he was too forward and she was accustomed to his reserve. Her feelings were a quagmire, did she love him or did she merely lust after him? Who could she ask for help? Not her mother! Charlotte? She ran from the church with a burning blush and hated his knowing she was agitated. She sat in the carriage to calm down while she waited for Charlotte and felt shaken and dizzy, by turns.

"Dear Lord, I cannot wait another week til Sunday to see her again." He leaped on his horse and headed for Pemberley where there was a pond that he dove into whenever he thought of life without Elizabeth.

It happened that Darcy's attention helped her family when he intervened in Elizabeth's sister's elopement. He had paid a great sum to a soldier, a cad, who wanted to marry Lydia, seeking a decent dowry from her family.

Even though the Bennets had a manor and servants, they were not rich and Mrs. Bennet worried herself to approaching hysteria twice a week because of it. The elopement almost pleased her because she felt a few steps closer to a marriage for one of her daughters. As it followed soon after, she was restored to bliss and good health. Now, only four daughters to go.

If these young women remained spinsters, they would live at the manor as old maids and the Bennets would be close to poverty.

Jane, the oldest, had a wise and sweet manner, friendly and open to people, liking them until they proved hateful, forgiving slights and bad manners, willingly. She had a disposition to admire.

Elizabeth, the second daughter, was another beauty, as well as being intelligent, dramatic and attractive to people. She wished to be called Elizabeth, but everyone fell easily into her nick name, Lizzy. Her mother rarely favored Elizabeth and scolded her regularly because she saw that Mr. Bennet adored her.

Kitty, the middle daughter, suffered as many middle children do, generally left to herself by a family wishing for a son. She sensed that her parents and sisters were bored with another girl but she was coming into her good looks and when she was not pouting and whining, she was sweet and amusing, and tried hardest of all the daughters, to be sympathic when her mother was having "her nerves" or "her vapors" or "her panic attacks", or whatever she was calling them that week.

The most troublesome was Lydia, the next to youngest, who did nothing but complain and try to cajole her parents into buying new dresses and hats from London for all the sisters in her drive to flirt and seduce the entire corps of young soldiers, so conveniently stationed in town. She eloped and married George Wickham, an Army officer and rogue-about-town, to everyone's relief and a bit of her mother's pride.

A fifth daughter was Mary, who was significant but often overlooked. She loved to be alone and enjoyed her life of piano practise and reading through her father's vast collection of books. She paid no attention to her looks, having sized them up as hopeless, and she was impatient with the upstairs maid who was instructed to comb her hair in a becoming style. Sometimes friends of the family would comment, "She is so clever the way she plays the piano for the balls, but if she does not improve her looks, she will be nothing more than a spinster school teacher." (Family friends, then and now, can be cruel.)

Mary detested hearing their condemnation but she did not fret for long. Her ambition was to become a prominent. English scholar.

Chapter Two

Since the Bingleys and the Darcys were married in a double wedding at the Chapel in Meryton, the two young husbands, brushing aside all their concerns about winter travel and listening to their hearts, set out with their wives to cross the English Channel to visit Paris. They had been huddling mischievousty together to plan their respective honeymoons, far from England.

Elizabeth and Jane held hands under the tablecloth at dinner, thrilled with the secrecy clouding about them and they were completely bewildered about where they were headed after the crossing. William and Charles gave the girls instructions to pack three ballgowns, a riding habit and as many pretty tea gowns as needed to fill the spaces in their trunks. The honeymooners were definitely not on their way to the the sunny Riviera as winter coats, scarves and warm gloves had to be packed too, but the two men were so skilled at keeping secrets, it was not until they arrived in France that they began to pick up clues.

Right after the wedding ceremony, each couple had retired for a week to their respective manor houses in England to have some uninterrupted time to relax and become better acquainted. It was late winter and the large old mansions were hard to heat so it was necessary to cuddle in bed and do nothing more taxing than reading, sewing a bit of embroidery and making love.

The five dogs would not put up with being excluded from the honeymoon and moaned and scratched behind the bedroom door until they were invited in. It was not exactly an invitation they received but each opening of the door gave them the chance to bombard Elizabeth and William. Their body heat combined across their legs was downright boiling and Lizzie kept a small towel on the night-stand to pat her face dry after frequent dog kisses. She loved their affection, she loved her husband, and loved the honeymoon. William shared her enthusiasm completely, though he thought he should have first choice of his wife's cheeks for kisses.

....

"Dearest Elizabeth, there is something I must tell you."

"Oh no, I knew things were going along too perfectly. Is it terribly bad?"

"No, just bad. You see, I have spent my whole life in Pemberley and I am so used to it, I forgot to tell you before our wedding."

"William, TELL ME!"

"We have a ghost. We hear him moaning and rattling chains in the far part of the attic about once a week."

"Does he have a schedule, like every Tuesday or every Friday night, or is it just random haunting?"

"No, dear, it can not be predicted. Have I scared you? I should have told you sooner when I asked you to marry me."

"I have to admit, I am rather shocked."

"If this is going to upset you, I will sell Pemberley and find another home for us."

"NO! I adore Pemberley-everyone envies me, living here. I shall summon my bravery, and set my mind to adjust to living with a ghost. Does it frighten Georgie?"

"No she thinks the wierdest things are interesting."

"There, I had forgotten how strong you are, this may not be as serious as I feared. This is what I have been longing to do, I am always so busy with the business, I have not had the time to explore the west wing and the attic. There are several rooms that are locked up and with the ghost situation, I need courage to open them and enter. I think having you beside me will make me feel brave."

"But how am I to calm you, can you not see me shaking? I think we would be braver if we did this with my sisters and Charles Bingley and my parents. (No, not Mama, she faints easily.) Oh well, now that you have told me let us get it over with quickly, but I must have some wine first."

"There is no heat in the west wing, we must drsss warmly. I hope this is not too macabre, perhaps we are worried over nothing, although a ghost is not exactly nothing."

There were poles hung with costumes in the first room and they looked antique and very dusty. William sneezed violently and went back in the hall to compose himself.

"These will be perfect for "dress up" when we have children and we could have a costume ball."

Lizzy was so distracted, she forgot they were close to the haunted area.

Two more rooms yielded old furniture, things that belonged in a museum. They needed repairs for torn cushions and rugs.

The fourth room was amazing. "I heard that one of my ancestors had a collection of naughty artifacts but this is overwhelming!"

There were tables covered with china dinnerware and vases and teapots. With examination, they saw they all had paintings of lovers in loving positions. MANY positions. Lizzy laughed, "I did not know there were so many ways to make love. Did you?"

"I have to admit, we talked about such things while I was at Oxford, but some of these lovers have to be double jointed. Perhaps we should study these for inspiration!"

They laughed so hard, Lizzy pounded the floor with merriment.

"This man was certainly obsessed with this pastime, I wonder where you buy things like this? We should set them up in a special room to show to guests when we give parties."

"Oh, I think these would be too strong for the ladies but you could take the men to see them after dinner when they like to relax and smoke cigars."

Another door was opened and William looked in first. "Lizzy this one might upset you, stay out here while I explore."

"This is it!", she thought, "There is going to be a mummy or a skeleton in there."

William was standing in the middle of the room and called out, "This is going to take all your courage!" "Lizzy called back, "I do not think I can stand any more of this."

She walked in and there was William, standing alone in the middle of an empty room and laughing with his teasing. She scolded him with a mirthful heart.

"William, I think this is the first time in history that newly weds spent their honeymoon prowling through a haunted house."

Chapter Three

William and Elizabeth set out for France with sunny skies over the English Channel and placid waters. He wanted to show her the paintings and statues lodged in the Louvre and since she had traveled only as far as London, he knew she would be as excited as he was to browse through the houses of Paris culture. Night time was reserved for the Opera, the Ballet, and saucy French Revues. Elizabeth teased him about their steady night life and said she hoped she would not wear her trousseau to threads. He answered that they would go shopping the very next day on the Rue de la Paix and buy as many gowns and bonnets and dancing shoes as she needed. "Who could have a sweeter or more indulgent husband?" Elizabeth thought, "A month ago I was being pinned into a cotton dress in a village dressmaker's back room."

They set out early to window shop on a cold and windy day and Elizabeth felt blessed with her new black fur coat and hat made of ermine tails. William wore a beaver collared long coat and a fur cossack hat. They had to duck into all the clothing shops to warm up and they bought something in each. William had waited to select a wedding ring for Elizabeth at this very shop, where jewels were plentiful and gorgeous and she chose a ruby surrounded with diamonds and William bought a gold band with a small ruby for his "Married" finger.

Out into the wind again and pocketing their gloves so they could admire their sparkling new jewels, William grabbed Elizabeth's hand suddenly and pulled her into a tobacco shop.

"I did not know you smoke. I love the aroma of tobacco. Let us choose something elegant for you like the ivory pipe we saw in the window."

A good reason William thought they should hide, was the sight of the newly wed Mr. and Mrs. Charles Bingley standing on a corner a block away with their heads bowed, studying a map. He wore a Cossack hat too and Jane had a new fur coat of a light chocolate color with a matching fur hat.

The elaborate subterfuge to stay out of each other's way was invented by Charles, the creative one. Elizabeth and Jane were such close sisters, the husbands feared they might want to honeymoon all together. The game, something akin to Old Wives' Play, 'was chosen to be on their own for a few weeks. It had occurred to Charles that you could depend on the Old Wives' for almost any sort of game, but none came to him, so he devised his own scheme.

How he would love to go to them and embrace them. It struck William that he was close to being the happiest man alive. His dearest friend was married to the sister of his beloved wife.

Sisters who loved each other.

He was an emotional man, though skillfull at hiding it, and he sensed a catch in his throat, almost to the flow of tears, but he did not dare go to the Bingleys, that would spoil Charles' delight in planning the secret.

Enough time had passed since the Bingley sighting and now he could smoke his pipe a lá Sherlock Holmes.

Eiizabeth had never had much money to spend on herself and her first instinct was to think this elaborate spending was sinful. She was determined to pick out the perfect gifts for her parents, her sisters, Georgianna, and, of course, the Gardiners, close friends who lightly supervised their betrothal.

The next day was gift shopping time and they made several appropriate purchases and then had lunch at a restaurant overlooking the Seine.

A return trip to the jeweler's was to buy jeweled earrings for each of the sisters and Mrs. Gardiner and a special necklace with a pearl and sapphire pendant for Mama. Without question, Meryton had never seen jewels to match these gifts except when the Queen came to open the library.

Kitty and Mrs. Gardiner would wear their new jewels to church and balls, Lydia had never owned anything so precious and told the Darcys over and over how much she liked them, and Mary would push hers to the back of her bureau. She would much rather have a rare book.

Mrs. Bennet removed her sapphire necklace only when she bathed.

They went to a restaurant near the Eiffel Tower and as they were seated, William saw the Bingleys at a table near a window. He flagged the waiter and asked to sit by the back wall to warm up.

"I did not realize you were cold, we should have stopped shopping sooner."

"Oh, I am alright, I always like to sit in the shadows so I can study the people at the other tables. I think you shall enjoy it too."

"Well, I am learning new things about you every day!" Elizabeth said with a look of curiosity.

"I think I shall have Frog's Legs Provencal."

"I am discovering new things about you, as well", said William, "But I am afraid I do not have an adventurous palate, and I wish you would order another entrée. To tell you the truth, to see frogs' legs on your plate and your lips would upset me."

He saw the Bingleys from the side of his eye and they were leaving.

"That was close!", he thought, "Now I can enjoy dinner."

The remainder of the day was frustrating but they still loved Paris.

The predicament was to find gifts for the men. Elizabeth thought they were universally difficult to shop for. Certainly, jewels would not do, the men on their list were small town types, not the sort to wear jeweled cufflinks, scarves were unimaginative, and bottles of rare wine would be hard to transport.

At last, a good hunch. They would like fur hats. They were not too showy and so practical for English winters. Cossack hats would be happily received.

They walked to the Louvre and spent hours examining paintings and statues. There were artists-in-training sitting with easels and copying paintings. (The Mona Lisa had a crowd) Elizabeth had not seen this mode of learning and the day after she returned home, she bought paints and brushes. She now had varied and valuable works of art gracing her parlor walls. She knew she did not want to be just a "Sunday Painter" and set up an easel before one of Pemberley's most beautiful "Still Lifes" and painted a creditable bowl of fruit. Now that she was going to have unexpected free time in her life with servants to do the cooking and housekeeping and gardening, she vowed to draw and paint seriously so that William would be proud of her- not that he was not as proud of her as a husband could be.

That morning, as Elizabeth was admiring a copy of the Statue of David by Michaelangelo, there were the Bingleys again! In planning their honeymoons, the two men were aware they shared interests and as they toured Paris, this was a problem. When they finally rejoined, and Bingley revealed the secret, he recounted the four mishaps of choosing tourists' favorites where they nearly collided and he pulled Jane away and hid.

"Oh no! There they are again!" William said to himself. He saw their backs as they walked up and down looking at a wall of oil portraits. "I know I am a pain, but please be patient. I feel dizzy. I must have fresh air," Dizziness was a good reason to run out and they did.

"William, I am becoming worried about you, what shall I do if you become seriously ill in this strange country? Shall I flag down a carriage to take you to the hospital? Where is the hospital? I hope they have doctors and nurses who speak English. I think we should stay in tonight and just eat in the hotel's restaurant so you can rest. I know! I will ask the Maitre d' to send our dinner to our room. I think you look better now, I shall stop worrying."

It was a rainy day and they stayed in bed. Conceiving a baby was one of their hopes for the honeymoon and they had a good start. Elizabeth wished for a boy to look like William. She had heard that the first child in a family usually took after the father, and she had seen this proven true with her friends' families.

If she had a boy, she could see how William looked as he grew through each stage of his childhood.

It was not long for the secret to be out. "What a relief! I have exhausted my reasons to move Elizabeth out of the Bingleys' sight and I would never have guessed this secret would be so difficult to carry through."

The next night he asked her to put on her loveliest ball gown to attend a dinner and dance at the estate of Pierre Perrier, an old friend from Oxford days.

Elizabeth looked around the ballroom with it's large crystal chandeliers and the orchestra seated on a raised platform. The dance floor was graced with gardenia bushes arranged for their superb scent.

The tall windows had small candles outlining them and the room could be subtly lighted or darkened by the footmen who were dressed in satin jackets and high, powdered wigs. The waiters wore satin costumes too and one would think they would overpower the scene with their beautiful attire but the guests were in tuxedos and exquisite ball gowns and wore jeweled necklaces and earrings and some wore crowns.

Elizabeth thought to herself, "I have come a long way since the Dance Assemblies at Meryton with my sister playing the piano for the dancers at the Village Hall."

They walked down the receiving line and she was stunned to hear people introduced as Prince and Princess this and Baron and Baroness that and with all the bowing and curtsying she wondered how the host and hostess could greet all the guests without dropping in exhaustion.

"Darcy! What a surprise! How are you?" "Good to see you!" "Wonderful! You have not changed." "Is this your new bride? Beautiful girl!" "Darcy! We have not seen you in years! How nice! Let us get together and talk."

These affectionate greetings went on and on, Elizabeth could see that William was an esteemed man. The Master of Ceremonies led them to a table for four and Elizabeth wondered aloud about their table mates but she did not have to wonder for long because there were Charles and Jane being led to their table! They fell into each others arms and could hardly keep themselves quiet for the sake of the other guests.

The secret was out! They could not help but laugh all through dinner about Charles and William's similar styles of keeping the girls out of eyesight. Charles pretended feverish dizziness in the Hall of Mirrors when he saw the Darcys approaching them, reflected on all sides. He planned the route mentally so that Jane would not see them suddenly reflected looking over their shoulders. Charles agreed that it was a brilliant one, but he had to say the next was a sure stroke of genius, you could call it nothing less. "I shall never forget it. We were strolling on the path beside the river and I saw you walking along the wall up above and pulled Jane to the water so you would not recognize us." Then Jane wanted a chance. "Charles told me to kneel down and study the water to see if I could identify the fish swimming about. This was when I wondered if I were married to a lunatic, and Lizzy I had your exact reaction to "The Dizzy Spell." I thought. "What if Charles has caught germs from some awful French plague? Should I take him to the hospital? I do not know where the hospital is and then I would need directions and I do not understand French. I thought Charles needed a good rest, so we had the waiter bring dinner to the room. I shall be so happy if our children have their Papa's imagination and sense of humor, but are a touch less crazy."

What she did not tell about was their cuddling in bed that afternoon, just the happiest pause in their honeymoon and it proved to be a significant time because their baby boy, Mark, was conceived in that very hotel, on that very afternoon and since he was the first son since Charles born on either side of the two families for a long time, everything he did was considered gloriously sweet, intelligent, imaginative, humorous and, best of all, he had his Mama's good looks and his Papa's fortune.

Elizabeth was thrilled to discover that William had become an accomplished dancer, thanks to Georgianna, and the four of them presented such a delightful picture, the other guests asked about them and thought the newlyweds were quite the most attractive at the ball. It had been such an eventful evening, the girls had forgotten to ask the reason for all the subterfuge and hiding. Charles replied that there was an ancient superstition that told of a method to predict the number of children a married couple would have. It foretold that the number of friends they ran into on their honeymoon, would be the number of children, plus one, they would conceive."

Elizabeth said, and she could hardly keep from laughing, "I have been listening carefully and I think it was very loving of you to discover this but I will wager that after tonight's party, Jane and I should go to bed and rest and prepare our attitudes to be the mothers of approximately thirty, plus one, children apiece. Have you two been consorting with gypsies or Old Wives lately?"

Their next destination was Venice, Italy and they were enroute to a sunny climate and a place that was new to all of them. The boat trip was a smooth one as it grew warmer and only Jane complained about a bit of seasickness. She did not know if she was prone to that upsetting malady because she had rarely been on the high seas. She wanted only salt wafers and tea. There was a long carriage ride to their destination and though she was looking forward to the end of her symptoms on dry land, her sick feelings persisted and now it was Charles' turn to feel frightend because he did not know the whereabouts of a hospital and he would not be able to converse with doctors and nurses who spoke only Italian.

They decided Jane had motion sickness and with canal boats the only method of transportation, the honeymoon was not the best for a person who threw up every ten minutes. Charles was terribly nervous, mopping her up with canal water and trying to hold her in a way that would be thought would be comfortable. He had to carry her into the hotel and she felt no better when she was tucked lovingly in bed.

Elizabeth knocked and Jane was so relieved to see her. "William and I had a talk with the Conceierge and he told us very confidentially, that your motion sickness may be morning sickness and you may be pregnant and that he will go personally to buy little salted wafers with garlic that seem to work best for Italian mothers-to be."

"I hate to have our honeymoon plans disrupted because of me", said Jane, "I pray these wafers help me and I do not have to go through thirty more years of morning sickness to create our family"

Jane rarely joked, so they knew she must be feeling better. Charles decided to stay in and care for her and was acting like a fussy old nurse, pulling the curtains closed for almost complete darkness and undressed her by candlelight, pulled on her nighty, piled blankets on top of her and arranged six pillows around her head.

"Oh, darling, please stop. I am just so hot and I really like that view of Venice from the window and do you see the Golden Dome and the bridge over the canal, I love Venice already and I can even enjoy it from my "sick bed".

They hugged and cried with happiness and if the conceirge's diagnosis was correct, they would be holding a little Bingley in their arms, some time in the fall.

Elizabeth told William, "I am so envious, how I would love to be in Jane's predicament, it is so romantic, discovering she is pregnant in the most romantic city in the world."

"Well, we had better rush all over the place and see the sights if you are going to be" morning sick too, you know, when boys are growing up, they are sheltered from all these pregnancy details, otherwise, the human race might fade away, I do not want you sick on our honeymoon, I want you to share all the wonderful experiences and the beautiful sights with me. I am itching to go out and find a boat that will take us past the historic sights and a boater who will tell us the stories and facts. This is the most exciting place I have seen and I wonder if I should buy a pallazzo, since we are here, we might want to give balls like the Perriers', some day." William was a sobersides and always told the truth, so there was a possibility she could be the mistress of an Italian palazzo.

William came up with astonishing ideas, Elizabeth was accustomed to people who wondered if they could afford a new roof.

Jane had to beg Charles to go out and be a tourist. He acted as if he thought she would die if he did not hold her hand every moment or spoon chicken soup into her reluctant mouth, or adjust her blankets and sheets and insist she eat salt bisquits.

In desperation, she determined to feel well as she did not want to miss a single Venetian sight and knew Charles would forbid her to leave her bed if she acted the least bit queasy. He was feeling so apprehensive, he thought the baby would break in her womb if he were not in total control of her pregnancy,

At the pier, he carried her down to the gondola and made such a commotion, he embarrassed Lizzy and made Jane unhappy. She sobbed in frustration and the boatman was so concerned, he paddled to the dock and asked them to wait while he went to the delicatessen.

"What is going on here?", Charles asked, "Since when do customers have to wait while boatmen leave to have lunch?"

But, in no time, he was back in place and smiling with pride. He had just completed a language course and now he spoke English.

It was so fulfilling to be able to talk to foreigners and he had always said, "A tourist in hand is worth five locals in the boat", and he sensed Jane's problem as his wife had eight children and acted like Jane at the start of each pregnancy.

"I took the liberty of buying some Mother Leonie's Buttered Salt Wafers for you. My wife said they make her "baby sickness" vanish." He received a large tip.

Jane was so bewitched by the beauty of the city, she felt better and ate some Mother Leonie's and was quite herself again. Up ahead on the canal, they saw a group of boats as if people were gathered for a special event and as they drew closer, saw a bride and groom in elaborate finery and six flower girls dressed in shades of pink. All were soon aboard a boat decorated with flowers and streaming ribbons and they rode just across the canal to a hotel where guests were awaiting them for a Reception.

As the canal cleared, they chose to sail all around Venice and met Lizzy and William under a bridge and Charles called out, "Thank Heaven, I do not have to hide every time we see you!"

Jane was so thrilled. "Do you see how well I am? I am not morning sick or dizzy any more and I can stand up by myself!"

With that, Jane stood up, bumped her head on the bridge and fell in the water. A man on shore jumped in to rescue her and in a few minutes she was back with her friends.

Charles was in shock and Lizzy said, "Charles, I think Jane is in danger, she is just not thinking right and I want her back in bed. I will sit and read to her so she is not bored. She is in no condition to be out sightseeing."

Jane put her her head in her hands and bent over and wailed.

"Sweetheart, do not sit like that, you will bend the baby."

With that admonition, Jane gave Charles a nasty look, the first since they had known each other.

After the girls were settled upstairs, Darcy and Bingley took a walk to the Plaza San Marco and sat to feed the pigeons.

"Darcy, do you think marriage will always be like this?

Women seem to need a great deal of care, well perhaps it is just when they are pregnant. Do you think it will be nine months of this? If we have a large family, will she be sick and dizzy for the rest of our married lives? God, I cannot stand this worry, I just adore Jane."

Darcy, though he had no frame of reference at all, tried to pull his friend from the doldrums and said he thought the best thing to do was book passage and sail home to England.

"Lizzy will insist on traveling together so she can take care of Jane and cheer her. They are very devoted- well you have seen all of that, and I think Jane will have a miraculous recovery when she is home again in Netherfield."

The Bingleys had to buy another trunk for their load of Mother Leonie's wafers and sailed back to England with great relief.

Chapter Four

Mr. and Mrs. Gardiner, who were related to the Bennets, had graciously invited Georgianna to stay with them at their home in London while her brother was away on his honeymoon. They had three beautiful, well mannered children who were Elizabeth's cousins. Almost as if to break their reputation of sweetness and politeness, they sometimes disintegrated into naughtiness and mischief and they took care of Georgie's visit in a somewhat wild way, loving to have her as a new audience.

In their usual well disciplined, charming manner they played ring toss and croquet and other traditional English games, but, and it always seemed to coincide with the full moon or the tides, they almost had to play "Gotcha." It was a matter of secreting into closets and under beds and jumping out at the maids screaming "Gotcha!" The maids could not complain, but their Papa scolded and threatened and earned a day's worth of quiet. For Georgie's enjoyment, they told her to stand at the bottom of a long curving staircase, and when she yelled, "Go", they would race down to try to win the game. First, Jack pinned up Diana's skirt so that she would not trip over her hem. (They always made these little concessions to safety for their trial runs.) Being almost totally unfamiliar with childrens' games, Georgie agreed to be the judge.

The race was won by Tommie, who broke an ankle and coming in second, was Diana who landed on her head and sustained a black, green, and yellow "egg" on her forehead. Jack, the game's inventor, decided not to run the stairs and hid in the stable for the afternoon.

Seeing them so bruised and aching, they were sent to their rooms for only a half a day and Georgie was asked to read to them.

Every time William, whom almost anyone could call "born with a silver spoon in his mouth," saw Georgie sewing quilts and darning for the poor, he complained to Elizabeth.

"Hush, do not act so grand! This is a method of teaching girls to sew and it builds character too. If they marry carriage drivers, or grounds keepers or missionaries, they must know how to sew and make clothes," Lizzy teased.

"Have you lost your senses, Elizabeth? Georgianna has a fortune left to her by our parents and she will marry a missionary over my dead body, they are eaten by the cannibals whose souls they want to save. Can she not darn socks for the soldiers on our battlefields?" "This was the only thing the Darcys disagreed about. They had been brought up, one in a palace, and the other in a two story stucco house. Darcy was lucky their backgrounds were not reversed.

Georgie had a passion for designing "Crazy Quilts" and she went through the big Flea markets in London and bought second hand dresses of silk and lace and satin sheets and then sewed the scraps she pulled apart to connect them with hem stiching and embroidered names all over them as accents.

Georgie led the children through the makeshift stalls and they returned with bags full of old clothes. Their bewildered papa was horrified until she displayed her crazy quilt and then after much admiration for her artistic pastime, he told her he would accompany them on the next shopping trip.

Oh, such tears and pouts in a drama of protest by Diana and Jack. They insisted they wanted to be all grown up like their cousin, and their Papa relented a little bit. He would follow them but was instructed to come no closer than fifteen feet.

William had begged the Gardiners to chaperone Georgie whenever she was out because she had grown into a beauty and he noticed she was attracting unwanted attention wherever she walked. He had broken her engagement when she was sixteen to his cad of a foster brother, who was after her dowry, and he feared potential suitors.

After a few forays through the market in search of special fabrics, Mr. Gardiner became so bored, he told hs wife he thought the market, which was in the area of Covent Garden, was safe enough and simply warned Georgie and the children to speak to no one.

He did not have a beautiful nineteen year old daughter and did not comprehend the fallacy of his attitude.

In the Darcys' coterie of family and friends, Charles Bingley was not the only expert at subterfuge.

Georgianna had attended boarding school and was brought up as a proper young aristocrat, sharing her classes with the daughters of European kings, diplomats and wealthy businessmen, learning the correct manners to suit nearly every occasion.

They were sheltered from society and were shepherded about London in groups for limited outings, dressed alike in black velvet jackets, long plaid skirts and tam ó shanters. They had a uniform distaste for their outfits and pulled their "real clothes" from their trunks when they were closeted in their bedrooms, telling each other wild stories, some made up, of their adventures when they were home on holidays.

Georgie had no treasury of such stories, she and her brother were still grieving the loss of their parents, and life at Pemberley could be humdrum, punctuated only by her piano lessons and a random ball.

With Lizzy's and William's marriage, she sensed a taste of liberty ahead. She realized a burning interest in men and romance and was annoyed with her brother's constant fear for her safety, her dowry, her reputation, her anything- he could be such a pain.

She had accused him of secretly wishing her locked in a chastity belt and he was amazed and angry and demanded to know how she knew of such things since he had enrolled her in a school directed by nuns. She blamed her classmate, Alya, the daughter of a Persian prince, who was a wealth of naughty information.

Now she was back in London, her favorite place, and with a little imagination and flair, she was sure she could have some adventures.

Georgianna gave others the impression of a shy and demure young woman, with eyes often downcast, sweet smiles and gentle reactions, but this was a studied pose. Her mind teamed with humor and mischief seeking opportunities to burst out.

One day as she stood at the rag monger's stall, a wonderful looking young man came to stand beside her and tossed several a pillowcases of clothes on the counter.

"There, Nathan, they are full of old ballet costumes, you will find some good satins and net and a few pairs of toe dance slippers.

They are a bit shredded but some young balletomane might enjoy a few pirouettes."

Georgie glanced slyly at his face and recognized him as one of the dancers from Les Ballets de Paris. She had attended performances with her classmates at Covent Garden and was thrilled with the dancing, especially with the men who sailed in leaps across the stage.

She felt a happy surge of courage and remarked, "I shall look all through your pillowcases, I love to collect silk for my quilts."

"Oh, Madame, do you sew quilts for these children of yours? Although, I cannot believe you are the mother of this eight year old old."

"You are right, they are not my children, they are my chaperones," Georgie laughed. "My brother married recently and while he is on his honeymoon in Europe, I am visiting with their family. He worries constantly that I might be kidnapped or talk with the "wrong people."

"Well, I am Tristan Vastine, premier danseur of Les Ballets de Paris, and I do not think I could be classified as a "wrong person." I spend most of my time dancing and wandering about the Flea market for diversion. May I know your name and the names of your delightful cousins?"

He took Georgie's hand and kissed it with her introduction. She gasped with surprise and pleasure as the children laughed and begged for cups of ices from the vendor.

Tristan announced, "I have spent the entire morning practising grand jetés and I have worked up a tremendous appetite and I think we must have some ice cream."

They sat all together on two benches as Tristan told her of his childhood in Saint Petersburg and his life as a touring danseur noble. He admitted to feeling tired and lazy some days and was glad to be spared great leaps and turns and could simply join the troupe in waltzes and glissades."

He broke away when it was time for his lesson, telling her to look for him the next day.

Georgie lay awake half the night with excitement pounding in her chest as she imagined marriage to Tristan. William could hardly object to a dancer for her husband, he was well spoken and had courtly manners and all he wanted was the life of a ballet member, he would not be interested in her fortune. As his wife, she would travel around the world and she might even make herself useful by mending costumes, and, of course, raising budding dancers.

She loved this outrageous dream and fell to sleep in contentment.

She made the children promise not to tell their parents she had befriended Tristan. They knew she had been warned not to speak to strangers so she accented the promise by informing them she had seen them slide down the bannister from the top floor and had watched them play with the Humbolt twins from next door, whom their parents disliked, and also, she knew Sophie Humbolt's "lost" music box was under Jack's bed.

These stated facts seemed to impress the children, just as Georgie wished and they were thoroughly pleased to be included in the deception.

The next day they followed along happily in the hope of another ice cream treat, and waited as she walked to the theater box office to enquire about the best seats for the coming presentation of "Swan Lake."

It was not hard to convince her aunt and uncle to plan a night out at the ballet. They had been at a loss to stage a proper excursion to include their children and their new neice, and the night of the performance, the children did an admirable job of acting, there were no exclamations of, "Look! There is Mr. Vastine, We know him!"

His dancing, with many high leaps, was breathtaking and Georgie left the theater with her mind wrapped in a reverie. She thought there was a good possibility of another night at the ballet. Everyone enjoyed it.

In the following weeks, their meetings at the market became a joyful routine and Georgie thought more and more of Tristan as a devine romantic partner. It would be wrenching to leave him when William's honeymoon ended and she prayed for a marriage proposal.

One morning she came downstairs late for breakfast and her Uncle remarked, "You must have been very sleepy- but we have saved some croissants for you."

Uncle Nigel always read the newspaper at breakfast and he said, "Here is a sad story. There was a terrible accident last night at Covent Garden. A chandelier fell to the stage and crushed one of the dancers. A Tristan Vastine. He is dead."

Georgie gave a cry in agony and ran from the room.

"Oh, dear, perhaps you should not have told her. It is a bad start for the day. Diana, dearest child, why are you crying?"

"I am so sad for Georgie, "she sobbed, "I shall go up to be with her."

Nigel was quizzical. "Is there something more to this than we know? What could it be? I am completely mystified."

Diana crept into her cousin's room and cuddled beside her in bed, trying to comfort her. She had sensed Georgie's love for Tristan, and felt sick with sorrow.

They lay together all morning, sharing the grief that must always remain a secret.

"Diana, if I had obeyed my brother's warning, I would not have this awful tragedy to carry through my life. I shall never speak of Tristan again and you must not.

I shall live my life in a way that would have pleased him. That is all I can do to honor his memory."

....

When she returned to Pemberley, she walked to the village for singing and piano lessons with the choir director and practised feverishly. William had given her the finest of pianos and she wanted him to know how much she liked it. She was in on a surprise for Lizzy.

One day as the newlyweds paused in the corridor, William said, "There is a secret about me that you do not know or would ever dream of."

Elizabeth though, "Oh dear God, he is going to tell me his ancestors were murderers or there is a curse on his family or he is dying a slow death. What could it be?"

She had inherited a bit of her mother's pessimism and hysteria.

He took her hand and led her to Georgie who was sitting beside the piano with a big smile. A polished cello was next to the piano and he sat down, placed it between his legs and took up a bow.

The two played perfectly – a well know piece by Bach she remembered from church services and Elizabeth clapped her hands with excitement. "Is there no end to your sweetness and grace and talent?"

"We have a plan," Georgie joined in, "We shall all practise together, with you singing, and someday soon we shall perform at family parties. Do you like the idea?"

"Oh, dear, my singing would spoil your duet."

"No indeed, Lizzy, together we shall make magical music. I love the way you sing, and remember, William has always said that your voice is the most beautiful he has ever heard."

"Oh my, William's opinion of my voice is clouded with husbandly approval. All I can envision right now is performing before the Bingley sisters. Charles' younger sister plays Chopin's "Minute Waltz" the fastest I have heard it and she is such a fine musician she could play on a concert stage.

The sisters despise me because William proposed to me. They thought he would favor the younger Miss Bingley and marry her. If they hear one of our performances with me singing, they would not be above spreading gossip that I am still an amateur musician and have no business singing with both of you. They would think up something terrible to discredit me.

Charles Bingley is one of the nicest men in England and he inherited the full share of the charm in his family and his sisters are like the witches that burst out on All Hollows' Eve.

Georgie giggled and William asked, "Are these women really that bad? I have wondered why they stay by themselves in Bingley's manor, I guess they are deservedly unpopular. Lizzy, dearest, you may do as you like about this performance idea but we shall continue to wish that someday you shall willingly join us."

She thought, "How can I resist such gentle coaxing? These two people have been unfailingly kind to me. Perhaps this would be a good way to repay them." Lizzy often pictured detailed possibilities about her future, and then she knew her mind was changing. William had a new and becoming dove grey jacket that he wore with a black velvet vest and Georgie looked adorable in her sky blue gown, the dress that made her eyes sparkle, and she would have a rose pink gown made at La Fleur for the performance. She would join them and just do her best.

Georgianna was excited about telling this to Elizabeth. "Here is another surprise for you! William goes over to Covent Garden when he is in London to play while the ballet troupe rehearses." Elizabeth's eyebrows went up with each new admission.

"You see, when I am at our townhouse, I like to keep my cello standards up and practise. Otherwise, I would never touch my instrument. I am often anxious about this and worry that my parents would have been disappointed if I never play it again. They were very musical and I had lessons every week as a boy and then at Oxford, I took some stringed instrument classes and it turned out to be a good way to meet like minded people. One of them is Col. Paul Fitz William, Georgie's guardian and my partner in our rice and cotton business in America. He likes his home in Savannah, Georgia and he loves to travel in the states. Here is another part of the story. My parents toured the United States and always thought of Georgia as their second home. That is why this sweet little blonde beside me is named Georgianna."

Georgianna blushed. She shared the Darcy family shyness and it piqued her to be in an almost constant state of embarrassment with William's affectionate compliments.

Chapter Five

There was a growing problem with Georgianna and she felt depressed. She realized William sought a husband who would love her as he did, like a brother, but he and Lizzy were often hidden away in Pemberley and she thought of her life as nothing but music, study and loneliness.

One dinnertime, as they sat in the candlelight chatting after dessert, she started to shake and weep.

Lizzy was shocked and put her arm around her and stroked her hair to soothe her as she asked, "Precious girl, are you sick? Why are you crying?"

William was aghast to see this emotion from a young sister who was so quiet and uncomplaining. Georgie dried her eyes with her napkin and tried to compose herself.

"You see, almost all my days are filled with studying and practising the piano and sewing my quilts. I have no one my age to talk to, remember, you told me not to talk to the stable boys, though they are jolly, and you said I must not smile at any men in town and the shopgirls are too busy to chat. Things are terribly dull for me just now. I have no friends.

When I walk home from my lessons at church, two kittens follow me, one is an orange tabby and the other is black with a white bib and four white paws. The fish monger told me they belong to no one. They act so hungry and when I sit at the green, I feed them fish from the cup I buy. I would like to adopt them.

May I have your permission?"

Lizzy teased her and said, "That is a very modest request and since you are William's favorite sister, I am sure it shall be granted."

William agreed but worried his dogs might not be enthusiastic.

"I wonder why the dogs stay away from you, my pack is not the friendliest group of animals, they are trained to be watch dogs and keep thieves from our manor, but they have their moments of liking to stretch out on our beds with us and two of them would lick the hand of any burglar who patted their heads."

Georgie felt content with the attention and the problem solved, and asked Elizabeth to accompany her to the village green to collect the kittens. They rode in the coach, each carrying a basket, laughing and chatting about their mission.

As they reached the green, two balls of fluff jumped on Georgie's lap and began to lick her hands to find the bits of fish she carried and then climbed on her shoulders to lick her cheeks.

"I have a feeling these two have a serious desire to live with us. Let us settle them in the baskets and drive home."

The fish monger donated a cup of shrimp to keep them busy and Lizzy asked if she had chosen names.

She replied, "This little marmalade reminds me of muffins, so "Muffin" he is, and this one has to be "Boots" for his white paws. They are not terribly original names but I feel comfortable with them. What do you think?"

"These are adorable kitties and those are sweet, perfect names. Now we can introduce them formally to William. It is a good thing you did not give them masculine and feminine names like Polly or Fritz, now we shall have to ascertain their gender."

"Oh, no, that shall be no problem," Georgie replied with a smile. "Harry, the stable boy, taught me how. Oops! I am not to talk to the stable servants, please do not tell."

"Look out, Georgie, these baskets are not the best cat carrier iers."

They were secluded for safety in the carriage but these kittens wanted adventure.

"Quick, get a hold of Boots! These marauders are not seasoned travelers. The only way to get them home is to hold them very tight, without strangling them. And look at this kicking!"

Each paw slashed and kicked and they had no intention of staying still. The next sign of cat outrage was a moaning that sounded supernatural and then a bellow like a mean dog's.

"You cats are impossible! We thought you would co-operate and enjoy being our pets-good food, bowls of fish, a variety of poultry, whatever little animal hearts desire."

That last, about poultry, appeared to have a calming effect on Muffin, and Boots looked over from his carriage-riding perch, stuck with his paw in some window moulding. He also appeared interested in the discussion of food.

Georgie said, "I think it would be fine to just leave him stuck there until we are home, it will be safer than the basket."

Things became almost serene. Women often slip into nursery talk when they sight a baby animal and this was the time for it.

"May I be your mumsie? Where did you buy your boots? I love them. I want you for my kitten sweetheart, let us cuddle up for the ride."

"If there were six thousand cats in the world, I would find you and you would be my most adorable dolly, Babykins, Wait til you meet our doggies! They are not as cute as you, except Rumpus. How have I lived without you? Precious Dollycatkins?"

Leaving William home was the wisest decision of the morning. First, the cat, whom he had not, as yet, met, hanging on the decorative Rococo moulding of his carriage, and leaving scratch marks on the leather seat, and second, his wife smelled fishy, and third, Muffin was chewing discreetly on his sister's neck and making small marks that looked like the kiss of a vampire. No one could miss a faint cat odor rising in the back of his carriage, but most of all, William would feel close to losing his breakfast, if he heard the baby cat talk. Men do not talk to cats and dogs that way. They say things like "Atta boy, Rex, Good show."

Two of the big dogs greeted them with happy woofs, but when they saw Muffin and Boots, they stood still in polite wonderment. Georgie ran to her room with the cats hanging on her camisole and buttoned into her jacket, then she loosened everything and placed them on her bed. She had to pull Plato and Falstaff out by their front legs and with that, she saw two more hurling themselves down the hall. They were all big dogs, except Rumpus, and there was a good chance they had never seen a cat.

First were two curs. (that has a bad sound to it. Mutts sounds nicer) These two, although the size of small horses, considered themselves Lap Dogs. The next was a stragelly-haired Borzoi, a Russian dog favored by Emperors and last, an Irish Wolf hound. They had sound pedigrees and were all fast friends. Dogs love people too and they think we are dogs, the special kind who pat and hug the others, and with their camarderie, they like to travel in packs and love diversions, like cats.

Lizzy had tried to befriend them before but they kept their distance and ran up and down the corridors for exercise. They adored William. He was always doing active and fascinating things around the manor and they shadowed him with their graceful lope.

The affable reaction to the kittens was unexpected and welcome. Lizzy thought she knew about dogs and expected some hostile barking and then back to their corridor activities. But the scent of the cats seemed to lure them from the far reaches of the manor. Plato and Falstaff stood immdiately outside of Georgie's door and barked and scratched insistently to be let in. It was as if they thought there was a big party going on and their invitations had been overlooked. Ceasar and Igor were confused too and they ran circles in a dog frenzy of excitement.

The ladies were alarmed. Elizabeth suggested "Perhaps I can hide the cats in the closet until William comes home. We can ask him what to do, he will know. But, there is still the problem of even trying to get out the door and calling him the minute he comes home." She opened it to just a slit and was pushed in easily to fall back on the bed. "Beastly Brutes! get away from me!"

The five dogs burst into the room and did a quick run-about of sniffing and snarling until they pulled up short at the closet door and howled.

"Oh, Lizzy, what can I do? If I open the closet door, they may go in and attack the cats, I know nothing of cats and dogs and their needs. I have always thought that cats do not like dogs and vice versa."

"Come and sit beside me, we shall try a prayer." In a while, the girls' calm demeanor seemed to puzzle the dogs and they came over to arrange themselves around their feet. They each wore an expectant expression that could mean they were not going to leave until they saw the cats. After awhile, they licked Elizabeth's and Georgianna's hands as if the girls could be won over in this wet and sticky fashion.

"This is enough", Georgie said, "I am going to act mature and take charge of this situation. William always says that he wants me to act more independent and it was my idea to have the cats so I must think of a solution.

I have thought of one. I shall let Muffin and Boots out of the closet and pray that they all become friends. There. Amen."

What do you think happened? Do you think the dogs took the cats by their necks and shook each one until it was dead? Things of that nature never happened at Pemberley. There could be an unhappy moaning ghost living in the attic but life there was basically sensible and cheerful.

(I forgot to mention the bouquets of flowers with fireworks tied on with wire that the grounds keeper found twice a week by the front gate, but I will have to tell you later, just a bit later.)

The dogs took turns holding a cat under his paws and licked and licked and licked. After this, Muffin and Boots stretched lanquidly and looked as if they had been soothed into unconsciousness. The prayers were answered.

When Georgie took a nap, she had the whole pack around her. They wanted to sleep with her too and the kittens took turns with their heads resting on her satin pillow.

William came in to have her sign some papers and he remarked that that her bedroom reminded him of the London Zoological Gardens. "I expected this to be a problem, the dogs are supposed to prowl the halls at night and keep us safe, but as you know," he said, smiling, "I can not say no to you and Elizabeth, let us give it a few days in practise and pray too."

They all passed the try-out period and the answer was yes- the cats could stay.

William made her promise to bathe each dog twice a week. He was not a complete push over, and he did not want to hear any complaints. (He felt a certain sternness was needed here too.)

Chapter Six

"Darling, I have had a serious talk with your sister about our living arrangements and her needs in a husband.

She said she is looking forward to a man who will be a father figure and a lover."

"She actually said that? Where has she learned such a term? That sounds like a pretty large order to me."

"We have to remember she has known almost nothing of a mother's love and very little of a father, as well, since hers was away on business so often. I try to act motherly, but I am not much older than she is and my mother is so overwrought and hysterical, I never think of her as a model. As for a husband, I think a man in his mid-thirties would be right and let us do some traveling with her and pray such a man will turn up.

Here is my second idea. (Am I not a creative wife?")

William agreed.

"Let us have my sisters and the Bingleys for a visit. I have not seen Jane and Charles as often as I had wished, and then, of course, mama and papa, and we could ask the girls if they would like to live here to keep Georgie company.

I am quite sure Mary shall want to stay with my family since Jane writes she is engaged to the curate at Collins' church. Next week would be a perfect time for a visit."

Although he did not crave another young lady at his dinner table, William was interested in a solution.

"I sense the talented hand of your mother in your genes!"

It was such a significant and beneficial visit. Jane was over her morning sickness and liked to describe all the fluttering and bumping in her stomach. Elizabeth was so envious, she had to feign joy and interest.

A magical change had come over her sister, Mary. She had been so plain and retiring with her studying and music practise and at the balls she would play the piano and eat cake. No one cared if she might enjoy a dance and she was a mighty convenient accompanist.

With her engagement, it was a clear case of the Prince finding his Cinderella. Mr. Collins, a minister, arrived one day at Longbourn, the Bennet's manor, with a young Curate to introduce. He was thrilled that his sponsor, Lady de Bourgh, approved of this young man. She loved to have these young men at Rosings, her manor house, and Adam Ames was an accomplished fellow with a delightful manner. He was not handsome but what did that matter?

It had not occured to Mr. Collins that this was a fine time to do some match making to help the Bennets, who were his cousins. In almost all matters of human relations, he was tactless and numb-brained.

Mary was smitten! After breakfast that first day, she asked the upstairs maid to fix her hair like her sister, Kitty's. But no, she would not have it just like that, she needed more softness and ringlets around her forehead and she discovered blonde highlights she had not noticed before. All these natural enhancements come out when a girl falls in love. And oh, how she wished she did not wear spectacles!

Late in the morning, Mary dressed carefully and posed here and there in the garden as if collecting flowers for a bouquet, then she played romantic music on the piano and he finally noticed her, asking about the books in Longbourn's library and discussing poetry and art, subjects in which she felt deficient. He told her he would go through all his books and send his favorites to her. (She had never felt so appreciated.)

Mrs. Bennet, who had a brief rest from her brilliant matchmaking, saw what was happening and studied the romantic situation with delight. Mary had a terrible habit of wearing the first dress her hand found in her closet. "Mary, we do not have a minute to spare. Go through the dresses we have in the attic, the ones that Jane and Lizzy left. They helped those two to find nice young men to marry. They may do some magic for you too. I love the way you are doing up your hair. I am so proud when people give me compliments about you.

They say that we have another little beauty at our house."

(Have you noticed that Mrs. Bennet had a less frenzied attitude about Mary? With two son-in-laws who were multimillionaires, she did not have to be so diligent in finding.

42

husbands for Mary and Kitty and could just relax and watch Cupid handle the situation.)

"Mrs. Bennet! I know what you are doing and I heartily approve", said her husband, "This young man is nothing if not a gift sent to us from Heaven."

Mary went out with Adam for tours in the countryside in Bennet's carriage, one they rarely wanted to spare, and the weather co-operated with sunny days. They had many weighty matters to discuss and philosophy and religion are conversational ideas that can go on without end and they were genuinely interested in them.

Reverend Collins sensed that something romantic was in the air and could hardly wait to tell Lady de Bourgh. A marriage with this bride and groom would shatter all doubts and he, in fact, believed that she would recognize it as one more of his very appropriate good works. He wallowed in her approval and was there ever a man who so thoroughly loved his job and his employer?"

In the case there might not be a forthcoming engagement, Lady de Bourgh sent Adam to Longbourn each week for two nights. She blessed this possible union but she thought it would be unseemly if they married less than a year before their first meeting.

Lady de Bourgh had to feel contented and in this instance, there was no difficulty in pleasing her.

Chapter Seven

There was a perfect day in May for a ride to Highlands for the annual dog show and breeding contest. Elizabeth heard some ladies discussing it at the market and she thought it would be an enjoyable outing for their guests. William remembered he had seen the poster about it for years and had been only mildly interested, but yes, it would surely be a lively diversion.

When the Bennets and the Bingleys arrived, there were nice things to notice and show. Jane smiled and held a shawl to cover her waist but there could be no secret about her pregnancy. She wore a loose smock over her skirt and she was a bit upset about her appearance. Lizzy noticed that her face was pale and her delicate prettiness was gone, and she would never tell, but she thought Jane's features were coarse. She remembered hearing something, probably an Old Wife's Tale, that if a pregnant woman's face looked different for the nine months, it meant that she would have a baby boy.

Jane loved hearing that and it brought a temporary glow to her complexion. "I think everyone would be astonished and thrilled if I have a boy, that way, Mama would not have to end her days doing some more feverish matchmaking.

There is someone who provokes me regularly. It is Charles sister, Caroline. I think she is jealous because she has no sweetheart. She is always asking me how I feel because I look so tired and wan, and I owe it to Charles to have a healthy baby-as if I am out at parties every night. I wish Mama would go out and find a man for her, I think I will suggest it. A man who lives on another continent."

Almost the instant the girls alighted from the carriage, Elizabeth and Georgie pulled Mary aside to congratulate her and admire her locket, a present from Adam with a little portrait inside. Mary had done a pen and ink sketch and her Mama said it was a good likeness. Adam had given her a cross with pearls too, and to all concerned, it looked like a serious engagement!

"Where are the kittens?", asked Kitty. "Shall we have to search the manor to find them?" Muffin and Boots ran out followed by five barking dogs, as if they had waited for just that proper moment to be introduced. She knelt down and a cat jumped on each of her shoulders.

"Do you like to share your bed with furry animals? There is no shortage of beds, it is just that we do not know what to do with them when we have company. They are so spoiled and they think they must have a human apiece to sleep with."

"Do not worry a minute, I shall take the leftovers. I love that gamey doggie scent", said Kitty. "It will remind me of my old mutt, Casper."

With the dog show to anticipate, Georgie was in the stable asking for advice of Webster, the carriage driver, who had never been faced with the project of quartering dogs in carriages.

"I think, Miss, we should take practise rides to town, back and forth and then see what we have to work with."

The dogs loved it. They had never been on a ride. There was no plan to take Rumpus along but he climbed right in for the trip downtown. Kitty had to stretch and grab to pull him out. Igor, the highly pedigreed dog of the pack, with his U shape body, and his high arched back, could not be arranged in the back and would have to be left home. He sighed and seemed relieved. He just hated being pulled this way and that.

Falstaff and Caesar were interested in the journey and for the practise rides, they jumped willingly into the carriage. Falstaff was an Irish Setter and Caesar was of questionable parentage but a decided personality. Igor would have been their only exceptional thoroughbred for the contest, but there were other qualifications. Georgie had the list. Caesar might be in the Most Amiable Dog group or Best Behaved. He was not the Cutest, but if Rumpus survived the journey hanging on the side of the roof, he was definitly a cutie.

It occurred to Georgie that her family's dogs were peculiar. She had been watching the assemblage of dogs and they acted calm, sophisticated and accomplished. One could look at them and know that they did not ride to the show hanging on the roof of a carriage, like a canine eccentric.

The audience of the Dog-Devoted was assembled, dressed in country tweeds and tartans and some were carrying pearl and diamond topped walking sticks. They looked like people who had come to the show with expensive dogs and the Darcys were sorry they had to leave Igor home. He was a majestic animal.

It was time to line up with the "prize winners" and Lizzy was elected to go first since the afternoon was her inspiration.

Falstaff had been watching the event with apprehension and he knew what was expected of him. He saw dogs lined up by the judges to have brightly colored ribbons tied to their collars. He did not want Anyone fooling with his collar. He did not want to walk slowly in a circle with dogs he had not met either and most of all, he did not want judges roughing up his fur and holding his head in unnatural positions.

When William came to put on his leash, he stiffened his body so that upright and sideways, he could not be angled out the door. "Let us forget Falstaff, if we leave him here he will not be going anywhere in that position he's tangled himself up in."

"Alright, sweetheart, this afternoon is just meant to entertain our guests, we do not have to try to win prizes."

Falstaff was trying to sleep and Caesar acted non-commital. He thought he might enjoy a walk-around with the very attractive dogs but then again, he could be happy keeping Falstaff company. Throughout his life, he had been patted on the head and called "Good Dog."

Something important was destined to happen at this casual outing.

Georgianna had noticed a striking man who appeared to be in his thirties, staring at her from across the ring with a mean appraisal. He was dressed simply, and for that reason, he stood out in the crowd. His style of walking in the ring with his two dogs though, was pleasant and relaxed, and he smiled often, as if he was having fun with his pets.

There would be glimmers of Fate's Will during that busy afternoon. (Only I, readers, know what will happen and thinking about it as I write, sends chills across my back and shoulders.)

Georgie wanted to draw Lizzy's attention to the man and said "Look at the way he walks, you can see that he has practised often for the show. His dog is the best, see- he's won the blue ribbon. He deserves it."

The dog's owner resumed his place in the audience and continued to stare at her with his nasty expression and she was so self conscious, she wanted to go home. "Am I too dressy or have I not dressed up enough for this event? He must be getting a perverse pleasure out of glowering at me." She could not help taking quick side glances at him and she was sure he was not just admiring her, so she took Kitty behind a post and pointed.

"Oh that one, he has been trying to catch my eye too. Just ignore him." Georgie wished she could be blasé like Kitty and decided to assume her "Rich girl having to mix with the common-folk" expression. She could look down her nose with the best of them.

Rumpus was impossible and in his usual contrary way, he started to kick and squirmed out of her arms to run over to the Golden Retrievers and join them in their walk-around. The audience loved him and laughed and clapped and he was, so far, the best part of the show.

The frowning man seemed to be an official and he came directly over to her and told her to keep her dog tied up and out of the area for the rest of the show and he did not want to see them there again. She had not been scolded like that since her Latin teacher ridiculed her before the class. The thing with Rumpus was an accident and the audience enjoyed the short break from the formal part of the show.

As she headed to the carriage, holding Rumpus in an almost strangle hold, he kicked and escaped again. This time she ran outside along the tent and she fell on her stomach as she nearly caught his leg.

A large snarling dog watched them and ran out to push Georgie around with his teeth, tearing at her as she lay in the dirt. She screamed and moaned as he dug his teeth in her shoulder and then her breast and was not so affected by her pain as she was frightened by the blood surging down her arm. She looked at it and her last thought was she had never seen such a bright red. Then she fainted and was awake only off and on for the rest of the day,

"Get away all of you, I am a doctor!", a man shouted.

The cur circled her until he was struck down and dragged away.

The doctor tore off his shirt and gently removed her jacket as the blood flowed from her wound. She felt ashamed to be exposed before the crowd, that had only stepped back a few feet, as they watched him tie his shirt around her arm to stop the heavy bleeding.

She was in shock but aware that someone was pulling hard on her arm and it hurt terribly though she felt strangely calm. Mrs. Bennet had hysterics for both of them.

"Where is her family?", the doctor called out and Darcy came out of the crowd.

"I think we had better take your girl to my house so I can sew the gashes. Please follow me in your carriage. I am Alex Wright. We must hurry before she loses too much blood."

Lizzy asked William if he thought the doctor would sew up the wounds with her awake.

"I do not know, but I pray she is unconscious."

They followed Dr. Wright to a small house with a thatched roof and a garden. Trellises outlined the doors with red and pink roses and it was delightful. Lizzy thought he must have a wife but there was no one beside him at the show, and now, an empty house, except for the cook, introduced as Bertha.

William carried his sister to a narrow surgery table and it occurred to him that they knew nothing about this Dr. Wright other than he was gentle with his patient, had nice taste in flowers and was in complete control of the situation in this medical sort of a room. Lizzy looked around and was relieved to see a diploma from a London University framed and hung on the wall.

He asked Lizzy to help him take off her bloodied blouse so he could sponge her clean and did a lot of preparation at the site of the wound with strong smelling chemicals and then he took out a long needle for sewing skin.

"That is IT", said Lizzy, "I shall be in the parlor."

He had not covered Geogianna with a sheet after the sponging, and Darcy had time to see her sweet, exquisite body. The scars would remain but they would not take away from her youthful perfection.

There were twenty stitches and, mercifully, she had remained unconscious.

The rest of the family and friends waited outside and the dogs had been rounded up after they had enjoyed a short run and exercise. Rumpus was "In the Dog House" and heard many wrathful scoldings on the way home. No one guessed that through him and his naughtiness, Fate had sent a Sweet Caress.

The Darcys would stay the night or until their sister was well enough to travel and the rest of their party were sent on their way with many waves and blown kisses.

Georgie awakened to see the three sitting around her and in-her confusion, she asked if she were still at the dog show. She recognized the scowling man and she thought she had been brought to him for more scoldings. Why was she dressed in a white gown? Her shoulder ached terribly. Perhaps she was having a nightmare at Pemberley. The scowler asked her to describe her pain and then he climbed on a chair to reach way back in a cabinet to give her a towel and shook a narcotic on it.

"This is Dr. Wright." William told her. "Do you know you were bitten by a dog at the show? He knew how to stop all your bleeding and this is his house, we shall be staying here until you feel well enough to ride home." He was very worried about his sister and the trouble she had brought upon herself.

"Where is the dog that bit me? What is he?"

"A cur, they no doubt shot him," said William.

"NO! NO!!, do not kill him. William, go find him! I do not want him dead!"

She was nearly sitting up and looked very pale. Dr. Wright eased her down and had Lizzy hold her in place. He took William into the parlor and told him with all the blood Georgie lost, it it would be dangerous if she became overwrought.

"Go back to the fairgrounds and see if you can find the dog. Then ask the grounds keeper to cage him until your sister is well enough to see him. I know this is a lot of trouble but I do not know what else to do."

His cook brought in steaming bowls of soup and bisquits and Lizzy held Georgie's head so she could spoon some for her.

"I can see you are very tired, Mrs. Darcy, Bertha will show you to a bedroom. I think your sister will doze and I shall stay with her."

He put the narcotic to her nose again and she relaxed.

"Do you live at Pemberley in Derbyshire?!"

"Yes, I live with my brother and his new wife. Where are they, have they left for home?"

"You have not been abandoned, have no fear." He pushed aside the white coat to take a close look at her wound. They were alone together and she had a vague memory of him undressing her and washing her all over with medicine soap. She was accustomed to the doctor in Derbyshire. He was elderly and so kind and helpful and treated her like a grandaughter.

Georgianna and Alex's situation proved the knowledge of psychology that claims a person who goes through a very painful experience will fall for the first person who is kind to him. Dr. Wright was so puzzling, and very handsome. She did not know how to act with him, though he was taking care of her-dutifully. He had been rough with her feelings and she kept returning in her mind to his nasty scowls and arrogance at the show, yet she wanted to kiss his hands and touch his cheek.

Chapter Eight

Lizzy took off her shoes and sank back into a pile of pillows and said to herself "No more dog shows, ever!"

This episode had the fine touch of a Guardian Angel and the Darcys would be eternally grateful to Dr. Wright. That is just the way these Angels work. You think you are in a dreadful mess of danger and then one of them arrives with help and stays just until he is sure you are alright.

It looked as if Georgie would have scars on her shoulder and breast but she did not bleed to death and they thanked God for that.

When a woman is exquisitely beautiful, but has imperfections like scars that show she has suffered and is vulnerable, she becomes immeasurably appealing and touching.

Dr. Wright moved her arm away from her body- very slowly and she did not seem to be uncomfortable, the medicine acted to help her through the pain.

She was asleep again and he sat with her and tried to read some Medical Journals. He found it impossible to take his eyes away from her. She was the loveliest of his patients and he wondered if she noticed him staring at her during the show. He hoped she would forgive his bad manners - sometimes he acted rude, though-he had years of University training, and he did hot have money to spend on stylish clothes and his etiquette was occasionally woeful.

Georgie woke up and was bewildered to see him asleep at the foot of her table.

"He is handsome when he is not scowling. I hope he shall not scold me the minute he wakes up. I know what to do. My wounds do no not feel so awful but if he acts nasty, I shall put my hands there and pretend I am in agony. He does not appear to have a wife, he has no wedding band and a wife would have been at the dog show.

I think I shall be pleasant when he is awake, it shall be wise to start off on a happy note."

He opened his eyes and stretched. "How do you feel?", he asked with a smile."

"I do not feel very bad, just hungry. Thank you for saving my life. You must have been angry to see me running after Rumpus when you told me to go far away."

"I do not understand how you could disobey me when I was wishing only for your safety. Young ladies your age should have enough sense to follow orders."

"Oh, my shoulder! Oh, it begins to hurt terribly. Please give me something."

Alex imagined snipping at her stitches in a few weeks. He thought he would have to tie her to a table for that end of the surgery.

He put a towel with narcotic to her face and it made her feel content.

"So you live at Pemberley. I have never seen it and I often travel the roads through Derbyshire."

"It is very well hidden. You see, I live with my brother, William and his new wife, Elizabeth. I could not have a sweeter sister-in-law. It is hard to find them sometimes, our housekeeper thinks they are often in bed. They want to start a family. I can hardly wait for some neices and nephews. There is a pond way in the back of our property and they go there to swim without their clothes. They do not suspect I know. We can see for miles from our third floor windows! (Remember, she was high on narcotics.)

My hair is all dirty and tangled, may I wash it?"

"No you shall not be steady on your feet, I shall wash it."

He pulled his chair to the closet and mentioned, "My housekeeper collects perfumed soap, I guess they have been waiting there just for you."

"Have you ever fallen from that chair? I think you need a librarian's step ladder."

"Sometime in the future, this is a modest office. Would you like lillies, roses, vanilla or blueberry?"

"I do not want to smell of food. Lillies would be nice."

He had never helped a lady's toilette, and he enjoyed it immensely, never having thought of it's intimacy.

He was wearing a loose white shirt, quite unbuttoned, and his chest hair stood at the third button in golden curls.

"How I would love to stroke him there, so much nicer than petting retrievers at the show" She laughed and thought whenever she smelled medicine, it would remind her of him. She wished for a shirt or a sweater of his to take home, smelling devine of rubbing alcohol and cough syrup!

These two people were falling in love so fast, they could not own up to it. There was a fear that one might reject the other. They were giving each other messages that were totally tangled in their first bad impressions, and there was nothing to do but finish on a businesslike note.

He told her to write to him when the soreness had vanished and then he would ride to Pemberley to remove the stitches. He wanted her to be very careful in the next month to move her arm slowly so the stitches would not be rearranged, and she would need help in dressing.

"I suppose you have many servants to help you with whatever you need?"

She hated it when that superior note came in to his voice. What was the matter with this man? He was hot and cold or awful, then nice.

He put a hand on her back and kissed the wound on her shoulder. Georgie drew back in surprise.

"Heavenly Father, what am I to do now?" She thought.

What she did then was lean forward and kiss his cheek. He looked at her so lovingly and longingly while holding her hands and kissing them, she thought that since he was in the general area, she wished he would kiss her wounds to make the pain go away, but, she supposed only mothers did that.

He ran from the room and collapsed on a chair in his office.

He was a man of strong morals and honor and in one day, they were tested and all deserted him.

What was he supposed to do about that little blonde temptress in the next room? She had done nothing seductive, She was simply lying down and looking beautiful and a bit sliced up. If anyone found out about his romancing, he would be banned from the College of British Physicians and the only job left for him would be doctor at the Poor House.

"Dr. Wright, will you please help me down from the table? I want to go home."

He assumed a non-commital expression and went to help her. He could hardly wait for all the Darcys to disappear, especially Georgie. He tried to look away from her face as he undid her fasteners and could not resist the touch of her soft young skin, and when he lifted her to the floor, his arms encircled her and he kissed everywhere within reach. She had an over all scent of a garden.

"My God, she must be possesed!" And he felt the Devil in him, as well. He pressed her cheek to his chest and wondered if she could feel the heat of desire in his heart.

"I think I hear the Darcys, I am going to put you in the chair and cover you while I find your jacket. Georgianna, you are a temptress!"

Georgie was only nineteen and had never thought of herself in that sophisticated term and, in contemplating it, she thought it would be an entertaining attitude to perfect.

"Mr. Wright, please do not help me dress in my jacket, have Lizzy do it. It is not that I do not want you to touch me, I like it too much."

A very practical idea came to him. Thank God, it was not an emotional one. "Your jacket is so stained. I have a loose sweater for you to wear for the ride to Pemberley. I am going to get it and rouse Bertha to make tea and warm scones for all of us."

Alex never disposed of her little torn, bloodied jacket. He thought that was all he would ever have of her and it kept her lilac scent.

Georgianna was left to reflect on her state of mind. Yesterday, Alex had annoyed her as he stared at her with a frown and then he scolded her, nastily, to get her dog and herself out of the dog judging area, and now she was resting in his home after being thoroughly kissed and hugged. "I am falling in love with him and I have known him less than a day. Dear God, why is this happening?" She was young and did not know that when Love comes, you do not spoil it with questions.

William and Lizzy were acting very friendly and respectful with him. "Where are they? I can not concentrate and I feel exhausted." I wish they would come and take me home right now! But, if they take me home this afternoon, I will not see Alex for a month. I want to see him every day! I think Lizzy would be glad to ride over with me now and then. She is a dear sister and always looking for diversions. I wish he would kiss me again before I have to go. Oh, thank goodness, I can hear them, they are up."

"Georgie, how are you? (it was so good to have a sister on this strange morning) Dr. Wright thinks you are well enough for a carriage ride. We were so fortunate that he was right there when you needed a doctor. Do your wounds sting? What do they feel like? Does it hurt just when you touch it, or all the time? Oh, Georgie, I am so concerned about you."

The patient smiled wanly and loved all of Lizzy's hugs and kisses and questions. Then William came in, looking pretty mussed up for him. More hugs and kisses. She noticed all this extra affection and thought she would stretch out her convalescence. She had never been rescued from danger before and she loved it.

William said, "I have news about the dog, do you want to talk about it? Alright? I found the fairgrounds keeper and he had the dog with him. It is his pet and of course, he does not want to destroy it. He was calm and friendly with me and no one can guess why he fell on you like that. The groundskeeper promised to keep him in a cage for coming fair events. What do you want to do, shall we ride over to see it?"

Georgie stared ahead in confusion and began to weep. Lizzy held her in her arms and Alex motioned to William to follow him into the office.

"If I can talk to you as a doctor, I do not think she should relive the attack. She is in fragile condition and there is no way of predicting how she would feel, why not leave well enough alone?"

Then he was off to the kitchen and soon reappeared with breakfast and tea.

"Georgianna, I cannot give you more narcotics. You shall have to put up with the pain of your wounds, they will feel steadily better, with short set backs, and I must tell you again, rest often in the coming weeks."

"Oh, so polite about it," Georgie thought. "Giving instructions so cooly, as a doctor should. He was kissing me a moment ago. I want to hurry home, no, I want to stay. I wish someone would tell me what to do. Do doctors kiss their patients to help heal them? I wish Dr. Wright lived next to Pemberley and came every day to treat my cuts."

Georgie was weak with the loss of blood and the narcotics and felt crazy with the torrent of emotions.

The doctor said, "I do not like your color, do you honestly feel well enough for a long carriage ride? Please, do not think you must rush away."

He thought, "I wish she was as white as snow. I wish she would faint. I want to keep her. Would the Darcys think me peculiar if I rode to Pemberley every day? I cannot leave my practise, it would be an hour ride each way. I would never ride so willingly. I wish someone would tell me what to do. I have never had such a beautiful woman on my surgery table. I hope she gets an infection, not a bad one, just so they would ask me to come with my medicine and stay awhile. I wonder if she has work or hobbies, oh no, surely; she has no work in that place. I am so hungry to know everything about her."

"We have quite a fine performer here," said William, "I guess she will have to go very slowly with practising on the piano. Georgie darns socks for the soldiers and designs quilts with scraps she finds at the Flea Market. She is quite an artist."

"What is her full name, Mr. Darcy, I just need it for my records?"

"Georgianna Rosemarie Darcy."

("How perfect, she is the escence of a pink rose.")

"Miss Darcy, please come into my office for a minute."

"I am amazed at this passion between us. I have never kissed and fondled a patient. I find myself rushing into someplace I do not belong. I am thirty three years old and I am rather content with the simple life I have here in the country. You are a kind of woman who dances at balls and has jewels to wear to them and servants to help her dress. I cannot provide things like that. You need a Prince to marry."

"I think your judgement of me is insulting! Stay in the country, I do not need you! I shall never complicate your life again. Just remember my kisses- YOU SHALL NEVER HAVE BETTER!."

....

The Darcys were on their way home and Georgie held the pillow the doctor had given her and cried all the way.

Elizabeth and William exchanged puzzeled glances and she said, "I think you will like my news, Georgianna. Kitty told us our mother is in full accord and she would like to live with us. In fact, she was planning to take the carriage back just to spend a few days packing her trunks. Mary was touched by our invitation too, but as we expected she wants to be near her fiancé, Curate Ames."

"Thank you dear Lizzy, truly she can not return soon enough."

Chapter Nine

"I can hardly wait to have Kitty here." Georgie thought, "I have to tell some one about Alex or I shall lose my mind. If I tell Lizzy or William - I know what they would do- they would get the police after him.

He scowled when I met him and frowned when I left and in between he saved my life and we fell in love. Well, this is one man William can not say is only after my dowry. This one thinks I have too much money. I am going to think this over very carefully and I see two possible paths ahead of me. One could be a life as a nun and the other in the outer fields as a missionary. There is just no appropriate man for me."

The next day a messenger came and he brought a large bouquet of flowers from Alex's garden. And a note. Elizabeth and William were acting thrilled about it but they would never read the message, nor would Georgianna, because she took everything to the fireplace and fed it to the flames.

"I do not understand this," Lizzy whispered to William, "He seemed such a pleasant man and after all, he did save her life."

In a little while, she returned with Alex's sweater and threw it in the flames too. This smelled like a hospital on fire and the Darcys decided to take a walk to town.

With a loud "Hello, Darcys, I am here!", Kitty arrived by coach with four trunks and the girls ran to embrace.

After dinner, Georgie told Kitty everything and she remarked that she envied her "Dramatic Life". "Oh, Kitty, wait til see my chewed up breast, you will not envy me." Something came suddenly to mind. "Alex said if a man loves me he will not notice my scars, I wonder if he meant himself?"

"I remember a story that a friend of Lizzy's told us. He studied psychology at Oxford, and one of the things he learned was that medical care givers, like doctors and nurses often find that their patients want them to act like loving parents. Alex is too young and inexperienced to know how to act with you, so he let go with his emotions. He might have felt guilty about causing your accident and was confused at what was happening, and he momentarily fogot his Hippocratic Oath."

There- I am just a little girl from Meryton Middle School and I can hardly believe how scholarly I sound."

They had tea as Kitty unpacked in her new bedroom and they agreed it was a perfect time to help each other. Georgie laughed and suggested she hang up her sign in the portico, saying "The Doctor Is In." Kitty was an intuitive girl and always rushed ahead, trusting her feelings.

"Are you still planning to enter a nunnery or the missionary field? I was so hoping to stay at least six months. Do you know that the novitiates in nunneries are not allowed to speak the first year? Barbara Conner from Meryton tried it out and she only lasted a month. But then, she is a chatterbox.

I would not mind being kissed by a passionate doctor while resting on a surgery table. And, luckiest you, You kissed him back!"

The next morning, Georgie was awakened by a clap of hands. Kitty said "I am so sorry but I have not been able to sleep. I am so frightened. I waited and waited to wake you at a respectable hour-is seven alright?

I have been listening to loud moaning and crackling. Is someone dying here? It comes from way down the corridors in the other part of the house. Did you hear it? Is it the wind?"

"No, no, it is not the wind, it is our old Pemberley ghost. We hear him at least once a week and we have lost some upstairs maids because of him. I have grown up listening to him so he does not scare me. I should have warned you."

"Oh, what can I do? I cannot bear the thought that some unhappy spirit roams the corridors, dragging chains or doing violent things like ghosts in plays by Shakespeare. I can just picture Hamlet holding up a skull and saying "Alas, poor Yorick, I knew him well."

"Listen! I have such a good idea! Why not have the stable boy move your bed in here? That way we do not have to share the animals. The cats are always here and usually two or three dogs. It will be our own 'Noah's Ark'."

"That sounds just perfect, to me, I have never had a special pet."

The cats purred and Plato and Falstaff snored, but that was nowhere as bad as a ghost moaning and carrying on and throwing pebbles at the window panes.

Kitty had a brilliant idea. Since Mary's fiancé studied for the Ministry at the University, he might know about ridding places of unhappy ghosts. She thought there could be no happy ghosts since they would have no reason to moan and wail in agony, so she and Georgie composed a letter to Mary to ask if she and Adam would come for a visit and discuss some strategy.

A week passed and messengers brought only business letters for William and large bouquets of roses with notes from Alex that she referred to as "those tiresome flowers" and "wretched notes." She took them directly to the fireplace and made a big show of burning them. Elizabeth witnessed all of this and asked Georgie to sit with her to discuss what she was doing.

"You told me that you were looking for a husband who would be like a father and a lover, and though we do not know Dr. Wright well, he seems like a good solid professional man and he is kind and handsome, as well, and he appears to be smitten with you. The gardenias he sends with the roses are imported from the tropics and I think it is sinful to burn them. I would love to have them to put in our bedroom. And also, Georgie, I wish you would not refer to him as "the Dauntless doh doh" and remember, he did save your life."

"Oh Lizzy, I do not want him. First he covers me with kisses and calls me his devine angel and he has never touched a woman so beautiful as me and then he does an about turn and says he could never marry me because I am just a spoiled rich girl with no depth and worthwhile character."

"I am so glad you confided in me." Lizzy answered. Alex sounds like your brother. When I first knew William, he proposed and then he insulted me and my family. I was furious with him and turned him down and then he just went about doing the most kind and thoughtful things for me, I could not resist him.

I do not have any advice, aren't you glad?"

The longer she was away from him, the more she thought about his wonderful tanned hands and the actual heat of his kisses and the way he put the vase full of roses in his examining room to cheer her up. I wonder how many children he would like. What if he does not like music? What if he comes to visit and William is in one of his shy withdrawn moods and Lizzy wears too much jewelry at dinner?

(Dearest Readers- I have always been of the opinion that if you care desperately to have your family make a good impression on your beau, it is true love.)

"I am in big trouble. I do not know how to have a thirty three year old lover. I shall save his gardenias but I will not read his distressing notes."

Kitty was a friend from Heaven. Georgie had so much happening in her life she could barely sort it out. She told her about all the kissing and hugging she had been a partner to in Alex's office and she was afraid someone would accuse her of seducing her doctor.

"Oh, listen Georgie, if anyone says you were too forward, tell them you were delirious. If you were undressed by a doctor for a purely medical reason, would you like him to be elderly like the doctor in Derbyshire or a young and handsome man like Dr. Wright?"

"I have not been kissed by any man since I was engaged to George Wickhan, your brother- in-law, and he was wonderful."

"What do you think he has in mind? Will he make a complete turn and ask you to marry him? Perhaps he over reacts to the sight of an uncovered young woman's body and he thinks yours is so overwhelmingly beautiful, he has never seen one so perfect. He has been stuck away in a country practise and he, no doubt, sees only well muscled farm girls. He does not attend balls, so he has not seen aristocratic women in low cut gowns. I wager Lizzy would not have attracted a millionaire like William if she were not so well endowed."

"Oh, Kitty, I could not have a sweeter sister- in -law"

"That is a lovely thing to say. Thank you. Lizzy and Jane are my favorite sisters.

Before we go to bed, I want to thank you, as well, for your invitation to live at Pemberley. Mama and papa are so grateful. I am "the middle sister, and no one knows quite what to do with me except try to marry me off."

The next mail brought the anxiously awaited letter from Mary and she seemed tickled with their questions. She had discussed exorcism with Adam and he said it was mainly a ceremony for clearing out evil spirits and thought they needed more of a "Service" to tell the ghost all is well and he should proceed to Heaven. The problem remained that they must have some knowledge of the ghost's identity and the circumstances of his death. He suggested they hunt all over the estate and try to find a tombstone and get a feeling about the ghost's anquish.

"This is nice, Kits, now I have something interesting and worthwhile to do as I recuperate. How do you think we should begin? We shall have to do it secretly so that William and Lizzy do not take over and run the whole show. William, especially, will find some reason to disapprove, but you cannot predict about Lizzy, she likes to have fun.

We must search the entire estate, mainly the borders, Adam writes that he thinks a gravestone may be imbedded in the earth with only a corner sticking up."

William rode past on the first day of their search on the edge of the deep woods and they called out they were hunting for rare types of ivy and fern and that was the reason for the baskets and trowels. (What an inspired idea to disguise their skull-duggery!)

He waved and smiled while thinking, "That sounds so wholesome and what an excellent idea of Lizzy's to invite Kitty to live at Pemberley."

They were out one afternoon dressed with dusty, stained aprons and wore dirty scarves around their hair as they knelt in mud to dig with their trowels.

A horse and rider approached and Kitty exclaimed, "Georgie, does that look like Dr. Wright?"

"Oh, no no no! It is! What will I tell him about his flowers and notes? I look disgusting and I have sweat running down my face and I am damp all over."

She had a sudden insight. It was perfect. She took a handful of dirt and spread it over her face and arms.

Now he will see that I am capable of honest common labor. He is certainly dressed up- high black boots and tan pants and the white shirt he likes to wear unbuttoned to show the curls on his chest.

He had a big bouquet of roses tied to his saddle.

65

"Georgie! I am so glad to see you! Did you get my notes? You did not answer, so I thought I had better come in person. What is that you are doing? May I help? I am Alex Wright and who might you be? Ah Hah, Kitty Bennet, I am pleased to meet you."

Georgie decided to say little so that it would be awkward for him, and Kitty jumped right in to describe their ghostly business, thrilled to become acquainted after all the tales she had been told.

It was a pure stroke of luck for Georgie's benefit to have Kitty present as a sort of chaperone, otherwise he might want to hug and kiss her with his idea of her as "Fair Game". Instead, in his usual scolding way, he told her she should not be carrying a basket on her "weak arm", and she should be favoring it.

"Alex, I am so glad you came, I had forgotten how bossy you can be. I did not read your notes, I burned them, and I think gardenias are too expensive and ostentatious to buy for a woman you are just "toying" with. Lizzy likes them, though."

This volley of contempt seemed to be going right past him and he looked at her with intense excitement and adoration.

That morning his dog had birthed three wonderfully colored English Setters and he knew it was going to be a spectacular day. There were no patients scheduled and he wanted nothing better than to see Georgie Darcy and Pemberley.

After hearing of their "charming endeavor", he gathered a bunch of twigs to use as a broom and slide through the leaves. Georgie was forbidden to work and instructed to sit still and "recuperate" (Here was the Doctor again, acting bossy, but she was secretly, very happy to see him and test some new wiles on him.)

They were at it for about an hour and Alex realized that it was the happiest day of his life. He was a curious man and liked to analyze peoples' actions and emotions. Nothing, not even winning a prize at Oxford, would make him happier than helping Georgianna Darcy hunt for a grave stone.

There was a sublime gathering of Guardian Angels clustered about the group that day and Alex was tapped with blessings…he found the stone!

It was a smooth one, almost covered with ivy, and it was sticking above the ground and needed a shovel to clear it.

"Come with me to the stable to find some shovels and your horse can rest and eat."

When they returned to the mound, Alex uncovered the stone and while it was thrilling to see, it was very hard to read. They brushed out the engraved letters and saw-

Here Lies Abigail Fentress
Beloved Wife of Hiram
Struck Down by Lightning
The First Day of September
1722

"Dr. Alex, you are a good luck charm and I am so happy to know you," Kitty gushed, giving him a kiss on the cheek.

"Just a minute now," thought Georgie, "Alex is my Love, and there better not be any more of this kissing."

She dusted herself, shook out her apron and gathered herself together.

"Excuse us, Alex, I must confer privately with my cohort." She looked full of mischief as she took Kitty aside and said," I think we should invite him to the manor for tea. I am hot and filthy and I want to jump in the pond for a quick swim. I shall wear just my chemise and bloomers. He has seen me in less, he is a doctor, after all. Shall you do it with me?"

Kitty loved the idea. She was always primed for devilment.

"Alex, we wish to invite you to tea. First, we must freshen up. Just walk in through the portico and wait for us in the courtyard."

With that, the two ran ahead tossing their clothes off left and right, ready to dive in the pond.

This was his first chance to see the inside of Pemberley and as he strolled through the door, he came to a courtyard with flowering trees and exotic bushes. Placed all about were larger than life statues of nudes, the kind Michaelangelo sculpted. The yard had the appearance of a combination of the Louvre and the Gardens of Rome.

"How do people amass money to build castles like this?", he wondered to himself." I shall act as if I have been to countless manors, some even better. I'll wager those two sleep on satin sheets and have solid gold handles on their furniture."

There was "A Grand Entrance" at the top of a tall winding staircase The girls were dressed in sky colored "afternoon gowns" and they walked down to him tying sashes and buttoning top buttons and fluffing their hair to dry.

Alex was brought up without sisters and his mother was plain and had no fancy fashions. (Do you remember, Dear Readers, that I described William and Alex as handsome men who were unaware of the effect their good looks had on people? Georgie and Kitty had been told, since babyhood, how beautiful they were and they knew they were enchanting. They did not even have to work at it.)

Alex had, literally, never been in the presence of such gorgeous women. They left him breathless for a moment.

Georgie took a bell and rang it to summon a servant. The housekeeper came in and she said, "Mrs. Reynolds, this is our friend, Dr. Wright," She curtsied and he remembered to bow. "Please bring us tea and small sandwiches, we shall be in the parlor."

Georgie acted shy at times and looked to be about twelve, but she was in firm command of proper manners. He guessed she had attended Finishing Schools and he was right- the best.

They sat in the parlor, a room the size of a rugby field and talked excitedly about mailing news of their discovery to Mary and Adam.

"Alex, do you realize you may alter the course of History? You must be psychic. Now remember to keep our discovery a secret."

"Why is it important to keep it secret?"

"We cannot explain now, but if you tell anyone, I shall have Dr. Elliot remove my stitches instead of you. (As if removing stitches was a treat to long for, and in this case, she was entirely right.)

Alex thought, "If only I could do just "everyday things" with her. Like this magical day. Digging for a gravestone is not for everyday but just cooking together would be a joy."

"Come upstairs to our suite. I want you to see our pets."

"That moment of mind reading made Alex feel as a treasured commoner invited to the Royal Bed Chamber."

Two cats were napping on satin pillows and Falstaff, Plato and Rumpus stood as they saw them enter. The room was decorated wonderfully and there were books everywhere. Georgie had scattered them to impress him as they dressed. They were romance novels but they looked like textbooks.

"William has us bathe the dogs twice a week and they smell of flower soap."

"Well, that solved a mystery. They must have the fragrant soap under their fingernails and on their bodies." Alex thought and smiled.

Rumpus was stalking about as if he wanted to look like a wild wolf, foaming at the mouth and yipping at Alex.

"Stop that! Alex remembers you from the dog show. The doctor is nice."

This occasion made him so unbelievably happy, Alex felt he might pass out.

"Well, ladies, I have to watch the time. I do not want to ride my horse in the dark."

They walked him to the portico to mount his horse and gave their hands with "Goodbyes and Hope to see you soons."

As he rode, he thought, "If there is a place in Heaven for me, Dear Heavenly Father, I must have Georgie with me after a long life together down here."

Taking several wrong turns with his preoccupation, he finally recognized a lake and took off his boots to dive in.

The water did nothing to cool his inner fires of passion.

....

Fair haired young Georgie, with her angelic face, her graceful ways and natural sweetness, would be puzzled and amazed to know the depth and intensity of love she inspired in an intellectual who was much older than she.

69

Chapter Ten

The girls were intent on composing a letter to Mary about their discovery and they wanted to rush right into their adventure and rout the ghost of Hiram.

A four day absence of Lizzy and William was ahead and they begged Mary to make arrangements for their trip. Lady de Bourgh and Reverend Collins were always happy to spare Adam if he had plans to stay at Pemberley and gather gossip.

The title, "A Permission", was created by Mary for the Ceremony and if the Ghost was connected to the woman in the grave, the point was to tell him where she was buried and assure him that she was in Heaven with her God and he could forsake the manor.

Adam did not want to simply walk to the haunted room and sit down to pray. It should be formal- a touching Religious Event. Mary thought they should wear either all black or all white. Black could look evil, so white was chosen to look pure. Crosses hung on necklaces were a must. They could march in single file carrying candles, or better yet, lanterns- much safer. If there was a table there, they might sit around it and join hands, but the best would be a piano, Mary could open with a melody by Bach, his music was so dignified, but it must not be long or they would lose their concentration. Adam wanted to be swift and direct. Then they would pray for the souls of the Fentresses. Adam would direct everything, he was the Producer and had the University training.

This is the meditation that Georgie wrote. Adam loved it and he used something similar in his further Divinity career. He routed many ghosts and became quite famous for his "Permissions."

As Georgianna wrote-

"We gather, in love, with our dear friends, to tell Hiram Fentress that the body of his beloved wife, Abigail, has been found to be three hundred paces to the west from the Portico of the manor, Pemberley. She rests peacefully because her Spirit is with her Heavenly Father. She grieves only because Hiram will not accept her loss and has wasted too many years searching for her grave. We gather to give Hiram permission to leave Pemberley and join Abigail in Heaven. We thank God for his gracious help. Amen."

Adam's letter of approval was waited for with great excitement and then the day came and they sat down to a big dinner with good wine- several glasses were needed to calm their nerves for dealing with the supernatural. They told them it was more like a mile to the grave site and the haunted attic had a round table with chairs, a harp and a piano and they dusted everything off. The piano had a busted up clinking tone and they wondered if Mary could sing á Cappella.

"No, No, Adam brought his accordian and will play an "Ariosa" by Bach."

As soon as it was dark and they were dressed in their "Whites"-a tennis outfit for Adam and long lacey white gowns for the girls, they made their procession to the attic. Their lanterns kept going out as if a Spirit was blowing at them but Kitty had matches.

The four concentrated so carefully in their commitment to this rite, they were unaware that a fifth was following them in the shadows. A dissident, a non-religious, a hater.

Mathilde, an upstairs maid, had taken in all of the mysterious activities and vowed to spoil them.

She took off her white apron and cap and slid along in her stockings, twenty feet behind, covered in shadows and looking like a burglar. She did not dare a few steps closer to the open door. It sounded as if they were having a success with whatever they were doing in there. Those girls were brave, she had to give that to them. Suddenly one screamed and ran past her. Then Adam yelled "Kitty! It's just one rat. He is gone now. You have to come back again for the end of the ceremony," and he ran to capture her.

That was that! Now Tilly had the "Goods" on them! The next morning she knocked on Mrs. Reynolds' door and said, "Those rich girls are having their fun with that Curate. They're doing bad things. They held a seance in the attic last night."

"Well, what were you doing there? These employers pay us to keep their privacy and I am sure they were doing nothing bad. Why, I have known Miss Georgianna since she was a baby and a purer, sweeter little person there never could be. You know, Tilly, the only reason you are allowed to work here is because your mother is my sister. I see all your pouts and nasty looks at the young ladies, as if you wish you could poison them. If you would smile sometimes, you might get somewhere in this world and would not have to be a parlor maid forever. I shall ask Miss Darcy what they were doing. I will not bring your name into it, but be careful, they may have seen you and I would need to send you away and there you would be in that awful flat in Cheapside with your howling brothers and sisters. Go on with you. Mind your business."

After serving them dinner the next night, Mrs. Reynolds said she had heard a lot of noise coming from the attic and did they know what caused it.

Georgie and Adam answered with the truth, missing no details. They told her they were frightened to listen to ghostly moans all around them in the attic but Kitty was more afraid of a mouse than Hiram. (Kitty gave him a kick in the ankle.)

"My goodness, you youngsters, it may be you have chased away that ghost for good. I must say, I shall not miss all his shrieking and hollering. Please tell the Darcys. I cannot see any harm done."

"A champagne celebration was held in Georgie's parlor with the dogs and cats sensing something was underfoot.

"If I hear anything from old Hiram again," said Kitty, "I shall never be able to sleep here. When I heard that moan-so close, and when I think about it now, I have goose bumps all over my body. If the "Permission" works, Adam, you could travel all around England, Scotland, Ireland and Wales. There are thousands of ghosts. You might advertise by word of mouth and charge for your traveling and you and Mary could see the sights and make money and marry soon."

Mary, ever the scholar, thought, "Goose Bumps." How can that be? Geese have feathers."

....

A horse and rider galloped up to Pemberley and he had one of Alex's "tiresome" bouquets tied to his saddle.

"Mmmmm, I love the scent, but he should not spend so much money. Georgie stood resting her elbows on a balcony railing and

73

watching in a dreamy fashion as Mrs. Reynolds greeted the messenger. She had become quite jaded with Alex's attention, something William had noticed in his sister, with annoyance and dismay.

The messenger handed over the note and pointed up to Georgie. The housekeeper left him and and could be heard running up the stairs and then she knocked.

"Miss Darcy, the messenger asks that you come down to read a note so that Dr. Wright will know you saw it."

Georgie laughed as she ran downstairs. She thoroughly enjoyed this romantic pursuit. She took the letter and tore it up.

The messenger thought to himself, "I like this job. I am making many pound notes and this romance is like a tragic novel. Wonder why the doc doesn't just give up. A pretty lass, though."

He dismounted and placed the flowers on the front stairs.

Georgie waited and then crept out to look for the pieces of the letter. A wind was scooping and scattering them but she found every piece.

Tilly pulled aside a curtain to watch and she swore. "That little princess gets fancy flowers and the stable boy gives me bunches with explosives tied in em, like that's all I deserve."

The odd bouquets were arriving regularly and William had a talk with the police.

Chapter Eleven

When the Darcys were on their Honeymoon in Paris and visiting William's University friends, he gave an invitation to everyone at the Ball, to come to stay at Pemberley.

He was a bit intoxicated and when he was awakened the next morning, he remembered the Welcome. Lizzy reminded him and said it-was a lucky thing that Pemberley had eighty rooms and enough satin sheets and silken down comforters to keep the hordes of guests comfortable and then, there were the battalions of cooks and butlers they would have to hire and the extra carriages and horses to be bought.

She laughed about it and shared William's belief that the Parisiennes at the ball would never cross the sea to visit them.

The mail came one day with an interesting question. Would the Darcys like to entertain some "Colorful Friends" of the Perriers, Prince Philippe and Princess Garnet de la Montagne? Pierre wrote that they were famous violinists who traveled with their piano accompanist, Anton, and gave concerts in the finest Halls in Europe and would be happy to entertain them at Pemberley before they embarked on a tour of America.

All the arrangements were swiftly made and the de la Montagnes were expected the next month after crossing the English Channel.

Philippe was feeling neglected on the boat ride and told Nettie that if she did not get him cough medicine from the Captain in a hurry, he would jump to his death in the Channel.

"Is that right?", asked Nettie, "You will jump and never play your violin or be seen again? I can only dream of such good fortune. Do not threaten me with your childish pranks. I could be in Paris at the Villa de bon Marche choosing my trousseau, instead I have to travel with my demented brother. It is only from the goodness of my heart because no one else wants you. I want to talk to my friends and I am not going to rush here and there following your directions. If you can not do anything but sit in your berth and chew your nails, think about practising your violin instead."

Anton walked about with Nettie like a little poodle, whispering that she was "a perfect Frenchwoman- beautiful even when she was angry", and to Philippe- Ecoutè a votre soeur, idiot!"

Nettie and Philippe had played their violins together as an act since they were five years old and, unfortunately, they were mediocre musicians, receiving terrible reviews and asked to play only because Philippe was so handsome. He refused to practise and stayed in his cabin instead, contemplating his impending death, either by drowning or the Plague.

He was a hypochondriac and used his imaginary sickness, with great success, to gain the attention of pretty women.

Nettie bustled in, carrying freshly pressed stage gowns and said, "I see you are still with us. Oh, terrible me, I forgot the cough syrup. What are your symtoms? Sore throat and localized soreness in your pancreas? To tell you the truth, Philippe, that really does sound like the Plague, please do not come close to me."

Whenever they played at concerts, the Claque, who were hired for the purpose, clapped with great excitement, shouted "Bravo and Encore" and then, on their walk back to the hotel, women ran ahead of them and tossed roses in their path. Anton plodded along carrying the violins and Nettie picked up roses-or carnations, if the fans were poor, and arranged bouquets for their room.

"Animals! I must have pink roses, not red! Red are so vulgar- they give me a rash!" He took off his tuxedo shirt and scratched his chest violently. There was no rash and Nettie was beyond worry about him. She had realized years ago that his "Illnesses" were a reaction to his mother's neglect and she carried a basket of bogus medicine and gave him teaspoons of this and that and rubbed vegetable oil on his chest and shoulders for his "rash."

She and Anton were having an Affair-so practical for their traveling time, and she was engaged to Baron Etienne de la Foret. It would be a "come down" to be just a Baroness after being born a Princess, but she loved him.

She and Etienne were invited to the best balls and salons in Europe while Philippe checked into a Hospital, had three weeks of medical tests and the attention of the beautiful and faithful nurses and he loved it as the best time of the year.

A concert was scheduled in London before he and Nettie and Anton settled at the Darcys' town house, and William and Lizzy and their sisters attended it with great expectations.

"Lizzy dearest, are we involved in a deception? Are these people serious? This may be a Vaudeville Comedy Act and they forgot to tell us." The applause was thunderous and Elizabeth said, "I think they are terrible musicians, but look at the women around us, they want encore after encore, we will be here til morning. Philippe is stunning and he plays his violin so gracefully, oh, he carries the concert by himself. We will never have to worry about their fame and fortune, the family is very wealthy."

The Darcys settled in one carriage with the musicians and the girls followed in their own.

"Have you ever in your life seen such a beautiful man?", asked Kitty. "And the way he moves when he plays? He is like a dancer. I am the most fortunate person in the World to be near him as a guest. Do you think the Darcys would allow us to shop in London for new dresses?"

....

They came home the next day from a shopping trip and the footmen carried large boxes in their wake.

"Adorable little kitten, did you and your angelic friend have a delightful and successful outing? I just love to see pretty women dressed up for parties and balls and you are the prettiest in London, including, of course, our beautiful hostess. Dress up and we shall have a Parisian style show."

William stood in the doorway as the girls paraded their new frocks. Elizabeth joined him and asked if he thought Philippe would make a suitable husband for Georgie. "He certainly is a practised charmer and she would be a Princess."

"Elizabeth, have you lost your senses? All we need is that Fop for an In-law, and a royal title means nothing to me. My God, I pray they do not stay for long and we must make an effort to keep him out of Georgie's path."

They discovered that was impossible. Philippe accompanied them almost everywhere they walked and drove, appearing to be a serious suitor, and it was plain to see that Kitty would like to be a Princess.

There was no reason to fear Georgie's attraction, she could think of no one but Alex and he was coming the next week to remove her stitches. At the thought of this, her body grew hot with longing to be with him.

She tried on dress after dress to watch Kitty's reaction and thought a very plain one in a wonderful shade of pink that had a jacket to be removed for light surgery, would be perfect. It looked inexpensive and Georgie would wear a very ruffley lace chemise and pull it down so Alex could work. She hoped to appear to be a woman accustomed to sophisticated seductions.

"Are you nervous about the pain or are you trembling about seeing Alex again?", Kitty asked. "Remember, he must lean very close to you, so wear your rose perfume too."

"Thank you, my dearest friend for your homespun philosophy and advice." Georgie laughed. She also planned how she would act with Alex and wanted to seem very calm and act mature and disinterested so he could not ramble into his "spoiled little rich girl" insults. He may never have said exactly that but she sensed his unpleasant opinion of her life and background.

She dressed very carefully each morning to look her best in hope that he would come. On the third day Kitty ran into their suite, pulling her to the window and said, "Look, he has a woman with him."

Alex acted businesslike and serious and said, "This is my Aunt Meg, she wants to assist me and afterward, would like a tour of Pemberley, if that is alright?'

Georgie stretched out on her bed as. Aunt Meg arranged scissors on a tray. She did not want to look. This medical visit was not going as smoothly as she had expected and she liked it less with every passing moment.

Philippe was very interested in the surgery and while they were waiting for Alex to begin, he came too close and had to be pushed aside. He was interested strictly from a medical point of view

78

and wanted to see if he could incorporate the attention to the stitches into his terminal illness act.

Alex whispered to Georgie, "Does that man have to be with us? Do you want him to see your uncovered body?"

"I am so scared, I do not care who he is or what he is doing, I just want you to hurry."

"Kitty, please go to the kitchen and have them put some ice on a tray." Kitty excused herself. She thought this was going to be too grisly.

He put small pieces of ice ahead of each stitch and it was not so bad. Georgie thought, "His hand on my wound feels like an embrace. I want him to make love to me."

"Did you like the pine sachet I sent?" Alex was intent on what he was doing and blurted out "I burned it." With that, Georgie started to weep and she was at his hands to push them away. "Do not do that! You are hurting me!" She covered her breast with her hands and said, "No, No.!"

"Please everyone, leave me alone with my patient."

"What is the matter? This can not be so painful."

"You burned up my gift!"

"You burned my flowers and tore up my notes."

Georgie was horribly upset and squirmed back and forth on the bed. He held her hands to still them. "Come on now, let us get the job done. This is just a job, not a romance."

She put her well arm around him and stroked the curls on the back of his neck and then she unbuttoned his shirt and traced the curls on his chest. Her hand found more buttons near his waist and he suddenly jumped up and said, "There, I am finished."

Please ring your bell for a servant; I must gather Aunt Meg and my carriage. Your scars will vanish and now you can go along your way, living in your castle with your maids, visiting London, and whatever else you young Princesses do to keep busy."

"HOW DARE HE?" Going off on that track again, I shall take care of him!"

"I am leaving next week for India. They need doctors there who will treat people as a mission and I have long thought of

79

becoming a missionary." He watched her as he told her of his plans. She acted surprised but not sad and shocked as he had hoped.

"You will be a fine Missionary doctor, I wish you all the best, our lives may be on the same course, I have considered entering an order of nuns and becoming a novitiate."

"Georgianna, No! A woman of your beauty and education who has so many people who love you?"

(OH, GOD! Why cannot I hold her to my breast and tell her of the desire I feel for her?")

All she did was wish him luck and tell him she might become a nun. He was devastated. The only reason he was going to India was to forget Georgie, he was no saint. He knew he could not make her happy. Distance and abstinance were the only paths open to him. He wished desperately to erase her from his mind.

Georgie took delight in telling him she might become a nun. She would not do it soon, if ever, she was no saint either, she just wanted the certainty that he knew she would not wait patiently in Southern England for him to ride up to give her a bit of attention and affection.

Kitty told her later that when they gave Meg the Grand Tour she admitted Alex wanted her to meet Georgie and give him her impression. She told them this girl was far too well bred for him an and if a marriage between them was a failure, she would be partly to blame. She had to be honest.

Georgie told Philippe she had no real intention of becoming a nun.

He suggested she join the French Foreign Legion and apply for an office job because the army was all male and an excellent place to seek a husband. She laughed and pushed him in a fountain.

Chapter Twelve

A messenger galloped to the portico and Mrs. Reynolds called the girls to receive a letter and a large bouquet of pink lillies.

"My dear Georgianna", the letter began. (I am not his Dear Anything!) "Please indulge me. I long to have you read of my concern. I am truly worried about your uncaring attitude for your wounds. If you do not follow my directions, you will not heal smoothly and you may always have pain in your shoulder.

It was wonderful to be with you and Kitty and I would love to learn more about your supernatural pursuits. Please do not burn my flowers. I choose them to delight you. Burning them hurts me more than you can imagine."

Your devoted friend, Alex Wright

A large statue of Cupid and Fortanna looked over her shoulder as she held the flowers tightly to her and wept. She said over and over, "A love note with no "I love you."

A waste basket in Alex's office was filled with torn paper and he had written the same message on each sheet.

"I think of you every moment of every day and I cannot do my work properly. I cannot force myself to book my sea journey. I wish we had not been together yesterday, it made my heart ache to be close to you and not allowed to embrace. I know now I can never give you the luxurious life you lead. What can I do? I love you.

Alex had been through many years of University training but one of Life's Truths evaded him.

The Best is often what we wait for the longest.

Georgie would not be rejected. She had received everything she wanted in life and she wanted him.

Kitty had been busy all morning writing letters to her family and she welcomed company. She knew all about the latest debacle.

"I wish I were more mature and experienced so I could give you good advice about Alex. I think it is nothing but chemistry between you. He is not my type-far too serious, and he is much older

81

than you. You really must answer his letter, he was so pleasant helping us look for Abigail's grave, sometimes I think you bring out some frustration in him, he must, though he will not admit it, crave your aristocratic heritage. Almost any man would be abashed by the palace you live in." Kitty, despite denying it, was a sage young Bennet, at times, rather like her sister, Mary.

"You inspire me, Kits, I shall sew a handkerchief for Alex and embroider his initials in the corner, we spoiled aristocrats are capable in a few of the homespun arts. I shall pen a note too."

My Dear Alex, (that was alright, it was just a meaningless salutation.)

We had a nice meeting, after all. I want to tell you about and I am enclosing the pattern of words in our Permission in the event you encounter any ghosts. This is the content of our ritual.

You are acting bossy with me, as usual. Think of me opening your note with a messenger sitting there insisting I read it. You are acting domineering and I will not stand for it!

You told me I would never do as a country Doctor's wife and yet, you court me with expensive flowers and visits. What do you want of me? I will not waste my time with a man who expects me to wait for him with hugs and kisses. I want a husband and a family."

Your friend,
Georgianna Darcy

A Messenger rode up to the Wright cottage and Alex was alarmed. Bad headaches had kept him in bed for the weekend and he was feeling confused and frustrated until he opened Georgie's letter and saw her handkerchief. He put it to his lips and smelled the rose perfume and saw his initials exquisitely embroidered in the corner. There was a fine fire burning and he followed an impulse and threw it in. Tears flooded his eyes and he could barely see. "Oh Dear God, I want it back!" The handkerchief was ashes and the perfume was heavy in the room.

After awhile, he read her letter. "I am only "her friend?" He burned that gladly and returned to sit in his armchair, crying and sobbing.

"I can not have her and she is turning into a little vixen to torment me."

There are not many couples in history whose emotions caused conflict then rapture and loathing that seesawed into intense desire.

Sadly, Georgie and Alex's relationship was one of them.

Chapter Thirteen

"Now that Georgie is unable to play the piano and sew, I have a good idea to keep our sisters busy. I was at the market and some of the ladies were talking about twins who live in the Mill. They give French lessons and their teaching method is very successful", said Elizabeth.

"Darling, remember the last idea you had after listening to the ladies at the market. About the dog show?"

"Oh, come now, dearest, this is entirely different. I would like to invite them to tea to discuss lessons for us."

"I will go along with that, send them a letter."

The Tremblants caused a commotion wherever they went. They began their identical lives as Babette and Nanette in Paris and were captivating girls with blue eyes and jet black curls who became more adorable with each birthday. Men loved their flirtatious manners. They were the meaning of the word Coquette.

Visions of their marriage to Royalty tantalized their parents, but the twins thought they were being optimistic. It would be next to impossible to find identical Royals in order to continue their lives together and so, they aimed for lives in the Theater.

An entrepreneur named, Edward Carl, who owned a Vaudeville Show in America, watched them coming toward him in London and almost stopped breathing. He signed them immediately to be the stars of his show.

The boat trip, on gentle silvery waves, was a treat for the rest of the troupe. The twins had brought enormous trunks with a new Paris inspired formal gown to wear for each dinner with the Captain and when they arrived in New York City, a seamstress, who had been engaged by Mr. Carl, began to sew their costumes and the theme was to present them, dressed alike, as Huntresses, Sailors, Nurses, Clowns, and Ballerinas. People in the audience, upon first seeing them, rubbed their eyes and thought they had sudden double vision. After the visual adjustment, the audience loved them and all the girls really had to do, was a simple "song and dance" dressed in their costumes.

Their dance, in Sailor Middies with telescopes, sung and danced to "By the Sea, by the Sea, by the Beautiful Sea" never failed to bring the house down and when they danced in toe slippers with identical movements, as "The Dying Swans", to music by Tchaikowsky, the audience would not let them off the stage. They danced it again for a minimum of four encores and it was the climax of the show.

(It must be easy to be a performing twin, once you get your act together.)

After a full career, many romances and much money, they traveled back to England and bought a charming home made of an old windmill, the only one in Southern England. In their small village, they were tremendously popular, always dressed alike, and when they saw them, townsfolk considered it a good omen for the day.

The tradespeople greeted them with "Bonjour, Mesdames!" (They wanted the twins to be impressed) and loved to deliver packages to the mill.

Each carried a large basket full of objects to be named in French and after that, there was to be no English spoken. Their teaching style was "Sink or Swim." One week there were fruits- la Pomme, la Cerise, la Fraise- and for Professions and Trades- le Fabricant, l'Artiste, le Banquier, le Concierge, and le Capitaine. They held up pictures.

The rest of the two hours was simply a conversation in French between the twins with gossip, apparently, because they often broke into raucous laughter and slapped their knees.

It was important to have their students roll their Rs correctly and they held their jaws and had them copy their tonque movements to say Tremblant. They loved to hold William's jaw to point out the proper way to roll the tongue. He had learned French at Oxford.

One Tuesday was the "La Famille" lesson and Nanette held up oil portraits of her relatives and named them. "Le Neveu, and le Cousin were trés attractif.

"Georgie, ask them where their nevue lives and that handsome cousin too."

"Why do I have to do these assignments?"

"Alright, Mesdames, ou est la Maison de votre nevue et, aussi le cousin, Lucas, ou est son maison?'

"She said le Nevue lives in a houseboat on the Seine and Lucas lives in, I think she said, a chimney.

You see, we are learning French and we should be very proud of ourselves. Let us talk about "The Permission" to rid Pemberley of our Ghost and what we did with Mary and Adam and we can see if they can control their natural curiosity when we tell them about it and stop speaking French."

"Mes Petites, Francais, s'il vous plait'", said Babette. Tell us about "The Permission", it sounds very exciting! I have always thought the windmill is haunted, we must talk more about this."

"Not in French, I pray", thought Kitty.

Chapter Fourteen

Anne de Bourgh, daughter of Lady Catherine, accompanied Charlotte's sister, Maria, on a carriage ride to Pemberley. Her Mother was a frightful woman of great wealth and power and her permission for the girls' visit was an astounding concession. She had come to Longbourn to engage Lizzy in a rude and nasty conversation before the Darcys' wedding, insisting that Anne and William Darcy had been betrothed since their childhoods.

Anne's mission was to observe life at Pemberley in great detail so that she could report to her mother. It was very doubtful that Lady de Bourgh would ever be invited to Pemberley.

In a stroke of luck, the Darcys were in London on a business trip, and Mrs. Reynolds, the housekeeper, was very busy directing spring cleaning, too busy to notice the comings and goings of a young guest.

Most people who had met Anne, remembered only her sullen and frightened looks when she was with her Mother. A year before, she had dark shadows under her eyes, and red blotches around her nose. Now she was smooth skinned and had pink cheeks and curly dark hair-another perfect English Rose. She broke into smiles at the slightest thing and the change in her was breathtaking. It was as if her glands had suddenly awakened.

On a lovely day, they walked together to show Anne the shops and the Inn and while the three were busy window shopping for bonnets, Anne walked boldly to the blacksmith and began an animated conversation. He was a handsome young man and Anne had noticed him immediately. He stopped his work at the anvil and stood to take her hand as she introduced herself.

The other girls came over to greet him too and ask if Anne would accompany them to the library but she said "No, no, I am busy."

After she walked back from town, Anne looked very sweet and mischievous and reported that Malcolm Bannister, the Smithy, had invited her to have tea at the Inn on any afternoon she was in the village.

Anne made it her business to be there every morning and afternoon, telling the Darcys she enjoyed walking and liked it as a healthful exercise. When she returned to Pemberley, her instincts told her to act quiet and composed. She promised her Mother she was still gathering information and impressions but after three visits in a month, there was a cloud of suspicion for her to handle, but she was up to it, she was in love.

The dogs and cats were all over the manor lawn, chasing toys and balls Georgie and Kitty threw for them. Anne joined the little gathering and said, nervously, "I have found the man I wish to marry. Malcolm loves me."

"What?, do you think your Mother would let you marry a BLACKSMITH?"

"This is the way it is, Mama has said that I should marry a Prince or a Duke or an Earl or, at the very least, a very prominent businessman. This is never going to happen and I have a large enough fortune to marry anyone I choose. I will marry for love. I beg you to help me. There has to be a proper time and place for Mama to meet Malcolm. I know Mama can seem like a scary old dragon, but she has a nice side and she is a good Mother, a very loving Mother, I am the baby in the family and I usually get my way."

Georgie and Kitty were enjoying the whole romantic project and they sat with the Darcys to talk over some plans. William said "Of course, I know Malcolm. He shoes all our horses." Lizzy interrupted, "Do you not think that a dinner party at Pemberley might be a risky affair? The last time I spoke to Anne's Mother, there was an awful scene and William, she has not forgiven me for marrying you.

I think she would be confused and taken aback if we extend this sort of invitation to her."

Anne joined in, "You just do not understand Mama, I will explain. She will be thrilled to come to Pemberley, under any circumstances and just wait, you will see a remarkable change in her attitude. Give her a pretty bedroom with satin sheets like mine. By the way, where did you buy them? I have never slept on anything so comfortable. I think I shall give her a present of some at Christmastime."

Lizzy and William were stunned with this change in Anne. She was charming and self assured and very determined, in a way, very like her mother.

Malcolm needed some proper formal clothes and Lizzy invited him to look through William's wardrobe. They had decided it would be a white tie and black suit affair with the ladies dressed in an assortment of Parisian gowns that Elizabeth had brought home from Europe. After dinner, the sisters (and Rumpus!) would sing a few duets and Elizabeth was practising a sonata by Cherubini.

It was becoming a gracious evening with friends and neighbors and Malcolm Bannister. Elizabeth asked "Do you think Malcolm is up to all this? Is he well mannered?" "Oh, Lizzy do not worry at all, I have had tea with him at the Inn and he knows the proper way to use the silverware."

Lady de Bourgh arrived in her heavily livried coach and insisted on a full tour before sundown. She had visited many times when William's parents were still living and thought it was even more splendid than she remembered.

Malcolm was seated across the table from her and he smiled often and hardly ate. She had a taste for attractive young men and thought he was very handsome. The footman poured glass after glass of champagne for the guests and Lizzy was afraid Kitty would give away the secret of the occasion, she had been giggling all through dessert, and as all but the Lady noticed, Anne had been worshiping Malcolm and batting her eyes at him.

Anne's mother was in a jovial and happy mood but she thought it odd that this young man was so well dressed but did not appear to be a relative or friend of the Darcys. "What can be the connection here?" she thought, and then she asked "Mr. Malcolm Bannister, what is your occupation? There was a collective drawing in of breath by the rest of the family. "I am a Blacksmith" he answered.

"Well, that is a most practical business, I should imagine, is it your family's?" "Oh yes, indeed, we are the only Smiths for miles around and there are so many horses that need attention and give us so much work, I can not continue my education. Someday I hope to be an accountant."

"Anne, darling child, do you know why I am so drawn to this young man? He resembles your dear cousin, Michael, the very same blonde curls and patrician features."

She was not, after all, considering Malcolm as a son-in-law just then, as she sipped champagne, and she became more and more enraptured.

Fate was busily engineering this Get Aquainted dinner and, if I may foretell, dear readers, Lady de Bourgh gave Malcolm the present of a tutor and in three years he became an accountant and married Anne in a stupendous wedding at Westminster Abby.

The newlyweds set out on a tour of Europe for their Honeymoon and eventually, Malcolm merely dabbled in his accountant business and they made several World Tours. Anne's dowry was a fortune and she became happier and more beautiful with every year. Even though her mother had wanted her to marry William Darcy, she still thought he was too serious and her Malcolm was by far, the more handsome.

As she gave birth to four Bannisters who followed them around the World, the grandchildren would thrill Lady de Bourgh and turn her into a sweet and contented old Lady.

Georgianna watched this episode with great interest and confided to Kitty, "Now look at the way Anne arranged her marriage. If she had been me, she would have my brother to contend with, William, who thinks almost no man in the Universe is eligible to marry me, or if one appears, he would be drawn to me only for my fortune. He does not mean to, of course, but he is insulting me. I lie in bed at night and I am so fearful, I begin to shake. I think, "Am I good, am I pretty? am I clever?, does God love me?, am I a good sister?, would Mama and Papa in Heaven think I play my piano well? Would they think I am lovable? I make myself wretched, I shudder and I do not sleep.

I have only Alex, who says I excite him, but he is a neurotic mess and keeps telling me why he can not marry me, mainly because I am a Spoiled Rich Girl and he detests the rich. Malcolm is poor but he has the right values. He and Anne love each other because they are kind and good and sweet. I love to watch them, their love is so simple and direct.

Kitty was a compassionate young women and she asked the Darcys to meet her in the music room while their sister was in the village for piano lessons.

They listened intently as she told them of Georgie's recital of worries and that it seemed to her she was in a dangerous state of mind.

Lizzie answered, "I understand completely and William and I have discussed this problem repeatedly and now I think I see a solution.

We shall concentrate on finding suitable suitors for both of you, we shall ask our friends in London if they are acquainted with some refined and eligible young men to introduce, and we might even travel to Europe and America. This will be great entertainment for us, as well as being educational. I love challenges and this will require some deft maneuvering.

We shall put our trust in God and we shall triumph."

Chapter Fifteen

Elizabeth knocked on Darcy's study door and called out, "Look, Darling, you have a letter and it smells of roses. I am very curious. Is it from a former Love, or, I pray not, a current Love, do you have some deep romantic secrets?"

"Now, Elizabeth, would you love me, totally untutored in the matters of love, I have my shy moments but I have not been cloistered at the University, or lounging about Pemberley watering flowers and swimming alone in the pond. This, I see, is from Fiona Warmheart. I have not seen her in a year and a half except at Perriers' ball. She helped me decorate Georgianna's suite. A really artistic girl, she's the sister of my friend, David, from Oxford days, do you remember her at the ball? She and her brother have bright red hair and freckles all over, no one could forget them, they really stand out wherever they they are."

Lizzy remembered Fiona alright, a gorgeous young woman who had a line of suitors waiting to dance with her, and a charming vivacious manner. "Oh Dear God", she prayed, "Please do not let this letter ask for a visit to Pemberley."

"Darling, you read it and tell me the highlights."

"Alright, she writes to ask if you remember inviting her to Pemberley to see Georgie in the suite she decorated for her and let me see here, she is going to be in London soon, and asks if we can have her. We are to write her in care of David."

"Lizzy, she is a jolly girl, I think she will be good company and Georgie will enjoy showing her rooms with a "lived -in look. Remind me to have Tilly scrub and polish and straighten, our sisters are not the neatest." (They often looked like the site of a tornado dusted with cat and dog hairs.)

"Well now, this is fine. A week to ten days visit?"

"I am sure she will agree to that, Darling, you had better send the letter off soon. I remember, Fiona is a real delight. We can plan to take our carriage to David's house and bring her home."

After Elizabeth talked about the visit with Mrs. Reynolds, the housekeeper called Georgie and Kitty to the kitchen.

"Young Ladies, there is something I need to discuss with you. Miss Darcy, have you noticed a basket on the top shelf of your closet? It is pushed far back. Now I do not mean it is something malevolent like the firecrackers tied to flowers that appear at the gate, and I have to say Pemberley has had it's share of the macabre, oh, but oh, I am off the track, have you seen it?"

"No, it is too dark up there, I would have to carry a candle -I could fall off a chair as I reach."

"Well, it is something I found when I was cleaning with Tilly. I think the message is something you should read. I fear giving it to Mr. Darcy, now he is married. I just left it in it's place.

I am not fond of Miss Warmheart. She is a troublemaker. If you cannot reach the basket while standing on a chair, you might just loop the handle with a cane to guide it down. Come back soon if you need a ladder. Amos has them in all sizes. Here is the cane."

The girls walked slowly and gracefully from the kitchen and then tore up to their bedroom.

"Here, Kits, let us push the desk over there- that is the tallest piece of furniture and I can stand on it and reach with the cane and I need a chair beside it to help me climb. This should be easy enough."

In their haste and poor furniture arrangement, Georgie caught her heel in her hem, fell over backwards and cried until Kitty rubbed her back and soothed her.

"At least, I hooked it, let me see!"

A delicate, be-ribboned pink basket holding a note addressed to Fitz William Darcy, what a treasure! It reads-

Dearest William, I shall never forget our intimate friendship. Please think of me whenever you enter this room.

With my passionate love, Fiona Warmheart

The girls climbed in bed and giggled as if they could never stop.

"Georgie! Have I not told told you your brother is a heart breaker? Now what is our next move? I think our next move should be to destroy the note. Do you agree? I think this would put Lizzy in a terrible state to know that Fiona may have been in her bed." Although, ethically, we must allow William to see it."

He read the note, with some amusement, and said, "I think we should go directly to Warmhearts' to meet David and Fiona and help her with travel arrangements and see how many trunks she has.

She will be here at least two weeks, there is so much to discuss and banter back and forth and we may have side trips to Derbyshire to plan and I know Charles Bingley would like to see her."

"Trunks," thought Lizzy, "How long do such visits last? Is there a possibility this visit will stretch to many months? William's excitement about seeing this woman is the way he acted when we became engaged." The occasion was taking on the proportions of a visit from the Queen and scruples demanded a battle plan!

Wearing her most becoming gown, a vibrant pink, was her first move. She had worn it to church and received many compliments.

"Are you not a bit fancy, Darling, for a dusty ride to London?"

"Heavens no, this dress is nearly threads, I have worn it to death."

William looked puzzled, he was so unaccustomed to thrift.

"Please have another made in the same fabric, I love the color on you."

Lizzy had sent an Emergency Letter to Jane and begged her to concoct some method to cope with Miss Warmheart. Jane was thought to be the most sensitive Bennet and the family sought her to evaluate complicated and potentially dangerous situations.

This approaching visit, and I think all of you will agree, was a DANGEROUS SITUATION.

"Lizzy, Dearest", wrote Jane, "You may fear danger where none exists. William Darcy is not a man who would flaunt a former lover in front of his wife. I think his welcoming manner in reacting to her visit is just in an "Old Friends" sort of a way, remember Fiona is coming to Pemberley because she had an invitation from William at the ball and she loves the Manor, everyone does.

Now if she is as beautiful as you say, she will have a very confident way about her and no doubt, she is very comfortable with her style of impressing men. This is the mood you must sustain-

concentrate on this give her a warm hug and kiss in London and act as if you have no one and nothing to fear. Catch William's eye often and give him sweet little confidential glances, that way, he will smile back and you will seem like passionate newlyweds, which, of course, is what you are.

It will not hurt if you pay warm attention to her brother to make William a bit jealous while you are at Warmhearts'.

This shall put him a bit "off center", always a good safe place for a husband to be. Then, off to Pemberley. Ask her questions and give her many compliments on her fashions and the decorating she did for William.

If you were jealous about their former relationship, you would act distressed. This is the way she wants you to feel. She is expecting William to fall in love with her,

You will confuse her. You will seem to be, almost without effort, the loveliest and most enthusiastic of new wives, secure in her husband's love. I think Fiona is the kind of vamp who enjoys upsetting married couples. Your sweet patient attitude will defeat her.

If Charles can spare me, and I think he deserves a vacation from pregnant and complaining me, I know it will be fascinating to see this vamping Fiona Warmheart in action. Is that her real name? I can not believe it, it sounds like the name of a Cabaret singer."

Jane was laughing all through this "Advice Missle" with her astute, though amateur, psychology."

"I am sure you shall have everything in tight control and I look forward to my visit with great joy!"

Within three days, Jane and Mary were on their way, driven right to the doorstep of the manor. Mary felt she could be away from Adam for no more than four days or he might go into a decline, but she could not pass up this opportunity to watch the Family Drama unfold.

They were welcomed to Pemberley by William, Elizabeth and Fiona. It was almost as if she was practising this gesture for the day she would take over as the Mistress of the Manor.

Later Mary remarked while holding her hands to hide her grin, "One would think she would realize we were up to something with this sudden visit and the way we stare and frown at her."

Mary invited Fiona to sit with her in the parlor as she examined the Philosophy of Aristotle when he spoke before the masses at the ancient theater in Greece, and ask how she felt about the Roman invasion of France, led by Charlemagne in 812.

Mary was revered as the Intellectual of the family and was most admired for the way she always walked about reading books from her father's library, even at the dinner table.

When she was forced to be with someone she disliked, she made up History to impress them.

Jane and Mary congratulated each other on recognizing Husband Thievery when they saw it. "(Oh, that is a good term, I must remember to tell it to Adam.)" While William and Lizzy were shopping for groceries in town, they took Fiona upstairs to see Georgie's rooms.

"Oh, I just love the southern views from the windows, they are what made me certain I would enjoy decorating the suite. Darcy and I made several trips to London to choose the furniture at the big Family Market. It was wonderful fun, we have almost the same taste. Is that a chip on the desk? It looks as if it has been dragged around. Really girls, do you not know that you have the finest hand carved pieces from India right here? You should show them more respect. Did your parents not teach you to take care of nice things?"

Georgie replied, "When I was three and one half, my Mama taught me the difference in Islamic and Tibetan art. Then when I was four, I begged for a Chinese Prayer Rug."

"I like the size of the closet with the poles to hang dresses and coats on and the three shelves above with the milliners' head forms to hold pretty hats. I always leave a little basket with comments about the nice experiences I had doing the decorating job. Did you happen to find my small basket on the top shelf, tied with pink ribbon?"

Fiona had no appearance of anxiety as she questioned the girls. Instead, a look of mischief stole across her face. She had some scruples, after all, and undaunted, she went ahead and said, "Now you know this is important to me, just a subtle link to Darcy and his sister.

Here, help me push this desk over, it is the highest piece of furniture, and I will put the chair beside it to help me climb." She was taller than Georgie, but as she rummaged a bit, deep into the dark shelf, she said, "Well, no success, I think the upstairs maid did some spring cleaning."

Georgie was beside the desk in case Fiona caught her hem on the way down and she did and landed in Kitty's arms.

"We will promise to acknowledge the basket if it turns up in a Pemberley attic."

"Just another thought, as I see you with this royal blue and daffodil yellow as I designed it, I think your blonde beauty deserves more of a pastel combination. A bright pink with fir green-Oh, so perfect! Now, Georgie, I would like you to write to tell me when William and Lizzy are away on a trip, then I can come with my fabric and paint samples and do it all over as a surprise."

Her back was turned and Jane whispered to Georgie. "This woman is a raging schemer. She said her baskets are "subtle links" to her clients- about as subtle as hanging a portrait of" Fiona and Darcy in an Embrace." She thinks redecorating the suite will give her time to recapture William's heart."

Fiona came away from admiring the window's view and announced, "When I see a piece of furniture or a little ornament I like that "Speaks to me", I buy it and store it away until it is right for one of my decorating schemes."

"What do you mean, it speaks to you?" Mary asked.

It says, "Fiona, your stunning good taste will be admired by all who see this room."

There was a raising of eyebrows from the group hearing the boasting.

"I have an artistic reputation to uphold all over Great Britain and I have never had a disappointed client."

"Just a minute now!", cried Georgie, "I like my blue and daffodil room, I fell in love with it the minute I saw it. It SPOKE TO ME. You are going to have your first disappointed client. I do not think it is a preposterous color scheme. I have been collecting pillows and bureau scarves wherever I go and I like it and Kitty does, as well. We are contented."

Fiona stomped out the door and was not missed as she spent the rest of the day sulking and refusing invitations to dinner and supper. She engrossed herself in composing a letter to her brother and it concerned the intolerable time she was suffering at Pemberley with four women bossing her and saying frightful things about her decorating and to add to that, she wrote that Darcy's wife was a Drone and she had no opportunities to chat with him and reminisce.

She sent the letter and then she felt she had some control of the visit. She had wanted to become acquainted with Elizabeth and study her wifely style for future planning and the days revealed that Lizzy was bound to drive Darcy crazy with her nonsensical, ceaseless chatter. She gave the marriage a year more at the outset and she had meddled in enough couples' lives to know the signs of destruction. It was a delicious hobby of hers.

Darcy noted immediately after Fiona's arrival that there was some dangerous discontent afoot. He was pleased that Lizzy was making a great effort to be charming and hospitable, but she talked incessantly, except when they were alone, and then she would fall on the sofa in seeming exhaustion, or stretch out on a bed with a pillow over her face so she did not have to answer him.

A note to Jane appeared to have gathered her with Mary for a quick visit at Pemberley. He doubted that Jane's absence would be a happy time for Charles Bingley, and Mary's Jason with his enthusiastic need for her almost every day.

He feared bringing this up with Lizzy for a quarrel might ensue and that would be rude for Fiona to see. He had been studying her and wondered what she had in mind with her flirtatious glances. She had been just like that when they decorated Georgie's room. He was not in love with her then and he suspected she adored Pemberley and his fortune. That last time together was strictly a brother and sister visit. Now on top of all this, Jane and Mary were whispering and giggling behind corners and he had to admit that his new family was, at times, complicated and uncontrollable.

How he wished he could take his carriage and deliver Fiona personally to her brother but he thought he should be quiet and pray for relief from these women.

"Dear God, it would be so good to hunt with Bingley or gamble at the casino."

His decision to keep still and bide his time was the wisest. He had many times put his trust in God and an answer came readily and thankfully in the mail.

David Warmheart sent a letter to Fiona telling her their Aunt and Uncle Roundright were in London, briefly, and could she pack and return in a few days? Elizabeth declined the ride with Fiona but Kitty and Georgie were bored and wanted to attend the Ballet.

It turned into a beautiful and exciting occasion with the Warmhearts and Roundrights. David paid so much attention to the girls! When they returned home they reported that they had met a Suitable Suitor and they had only scratched the surface of London bachelors. Lizzy put a damper on that one and said she would simply not put up with Fiona Warmheart as an in-law.

....

Darcy asked "Now, Elizabeth, what was that all about? I have not seen you so impassioned and vehement since the first time I proposed to you and you rejected me."

"William, my sweetest love, women have a sixth sense about potentional home wreckers. I saw that Fiona was a stunning beauty at Perriers' ball and I wanted to be sure she did not make some nasty inroads to our relationship. I have had you for such a short time and I can not bear the thought that other women may be lusting after you. You are so handsome and rich, I foresee a life of constant surveillance for me." She was laughing, but in her heart she knew it was true.

"Elizabeth, my precious darling, from the moment I first saw you at the ball in Longbourn, I knew that for me there could never be another woman to surpass you and I am thrilled almost every day as our life unfolds and I find another quality of yours to admire."

Elizabeth thought, "This speech sounds as if it was written by Shakespeare- I love it." Darcy had bought her many jewels, but she loved his compliments- sometimes borrowed from literature, but always the best.

Rumpus came in from his morning tour of the estate and jumped into Lizzy's lap. The dogs had kept their distance from

Fiona, with some inate canine sensitivity, and it was good to have them scurrying and lounging in the hallways again.

Jane and Mary had reunited with their men and Georgie and Kitty were spending time in their room. learning French vocabulary.

"Thank Heaven things are back to normal again," Darcy observed, "How did I ever enjoy that flame haired flirt?"

Chapter Sixteen

The Bennets had visited Pemberley during the Darcys' engagement but they longed to see the manor in early spring. The grounds were said to be of the first order in England and only four others were considered as magnificent.

Charlotte and the Reverend Collins were invited to ride with the Bennets and they set out on a sunny morning, passing flowering orchards and bright red roses tumbling over stone fences.

Mr. Bennet had claimed the barouch seat up next to the driver. He loved the view from on high- a pattern of farmland in squares like a quilt and he felt protected away from Rev. Collins who could find something or anything to chatter about for the entire trip.

Charlotte did some embroidery and Mrs. Bennet played nervously with her hankie and her buttons.

"My dear Mrs, Bennet, I must congratulate you on the illustrious marriages of your two oldest daughters. If Elizabeth had accepted my marriage proposal, she would have had nothing to compare to Darcy's riches. My Charlotte is a woman with inestimable good values. She has her care of the house and her chickens and, I must say, she seems gloriously happy- singing to herself all day and full of contented smiles.

We live closely to the Bible's instructions that tell us that wealth is no expedient to happiness and there can be beauty and harmony in even the most humble cottage. We have no servants because she is thrilled to take care of her husband and she scrubs and polishes our house to a shade of perfection. All we lack is children and Charlotte dreams of a baker's dozen. Dearest Lady de Bourgh, my sponsor at church, has promised me a larger house and it will be next to her estate on the most fertile rolling acres of Southern England and we shall have views of the finest countryside- as wonderful, and even surpassing, any views from Pemberley.

Your daughter, Mary, will have much to anticipate as the wife of my curate and I have to say that she is perfect for the role and could do no better than to follow my Charlotte as her model.

I am so drawn to her with her love of knowledge and music and she comes to me often with profound questions about religion and philosophy. Your Lizzy, I think, is the least studious of your daughters and I have observed that she cares mainly for fashion and forces Darcy to take her to Bath to drink the wholesome water. Everyone can see that she is a young and healthy person and likes to go there to parade through the Inns and the parks to display her expensive clothes."

"Oh Mr. Collins, you are in an unchristian mood! For shame! You are too hard on your cousin, Elizabeth. You make her seem to be a frivolous and lazy woman, why, I packed my suitcase just this morning with socks for her to darn for the poor and she instructs Kitty and Georgianna in practical sewing. She enjoys designing baby quilts for Jane's baby-to, be and decorates them so daintily with embroidered flowers in a most artistic style. She oversees care of the manor and is a very active woman. I am so proud of her and not just because she married a wealthy man. I think it was wise of her to turn down your proposal. They say that when first cousins marry, they often produce stupid children who talk too much. (Quick thinking, Mrs. Bennet, you scored!)

Now, Mr. Collins, I will listen to no more criticism of my Lizzy, we are going to Pemberley to have a wonderful visit"

"I am so excited", Charlotte said, "This will be a special time. Lizzy is my best friend and I miss her at the seasonal events in the village and church. She is the kind of woman who can have fun doing the plainest chores, like peeling potatoes and chasing my birds through the chicken coop to pick up eggs. Darcy is a very fortunate husband."

"Thank you, dear, I know Lizzy treasures you too."

They were promised a surprise for this visit to the manor and Mrs. Bennet had been trying to guess what it was all week. Perhaps a pregnancy! With eighty rooms in Pemberley, they had better start filling those bedrooms. Of course, Mr. Darcy can afford nurses and nannies, she will never have it as hard as I did with my constant stream of daughters. How I prayed for just one boy. I would not have to go through my tiresome matchmaking."

Mr. Bennet helped them down off the coach and having heard his wife's lament, cried "Mrs. Bennet, if you did not have daughters to marry off, you would find something equaly vexing to be hysterical about like finding only American masons to resurface Longbourn."

"Is that what I have to look forward to with our house or are you so cruely teasing me?"

"No, my dear, I would not dare to bring a little humor into our house, for fear you would go off into one of your week long snits."

Lizzy, Georgie and Kitty ran out to greet them and there were hugs and kisses and admonishments.

"Georgianna, you are prettier every time I see you, and Kitty I hope you are behaving yourself to deserve this stately home, and Lizzy, are you not pregnant?"

"No, mother dear, the problem is with Mrs. Birdslap's wonderful desserts, they are impossible to resist."

William came down the path, arms outstretched, to hug his mother-in. - law and Charlotte.

Rev. Collins began one of his tirades immediately upon alighting from the carriage.

"My revered Sir Darcy, why do you keep all this lovely land to yourself, it would be a marvelous park for your townsfolk?"

"I am pleased that you like it, we feel it is a privilege to live here."

His first sight of the carriage made him almost ill. He thought to himself, "What if it would be very rude of me to leave for business in London. No Lizzy would be angry. I suppose that a few bad eggs in the in-law family are just a part of marriage to be endured."

The young ladies surrounding Charlotte were almost dancing in glee, with news and gossip to catch up since their last visit and Lizzy had an engagement book that she had filled with questions that simply could not wait.

"Thank you, dearest Mama and Papa for coming so far to see us, did you love the spring scenery? What do you think of our fair village? Are you fatiqued after all the bouncing about in the carriage? And now, this was news for a town crier, are the Kingsmiths expecting another baby? When are the Lowells leaving for America?

107

Do you think Lucy Wade and Michael Killian will be engaged soon? No! They have seperated? Well, I just can not believe it!"

Lizzy and Kitty saw they were tiring their Mother and resolved to be delicate and asked no more until they were all settled in the house and served tea.

"Well now, Mr. Darcy, I have heard nothing but random conjecture about the surprise you have waiting for us and if it is not a coming baby, what is it then?" asked Mr. Bennet.

"Here, all of you," answered William, "Come and look at the back garden." He showed them the large maze that his gardner had cut back and manicured to be used for their games and pleasure. It was called a Labyrinth and was the setting for a game of chance on foot.

Collins could not let that by. "Mr. Darcy! I as a clergyman, must discourage this form of gambling in your residence. Do you not know this activity is almost always followed by drunkedness and prostitution.?"

"I am glad you brought this up, Collins, we must all endeavor to stamp out licenciousness and protect Pemberley from becoming a Den of Iniquity."

"As I was saying, the players are led into the first path wearing blindfolds and each placed at a different entrance and then, their eyes uncovered, off they go to compete for a speedy finish."

The Darcy's maze was known all over for the size and devilish design.

"Have you tried it, Lizzy?"

"Oh, mama, it is great fun, we have Kitty perched by the third floor window with a megaphone and this is very important because the maze can eat you up with frustration and makes you crazy to get out. When Kitty is asked for assistance, she calls out each stop and turn to help us find our way out In truth, we have practised our way through it so many times, we play it more as a time contest. Georgie and Kitty are so skilled, they need no directions and can run it in about fifteen minutes."

William added, "It can be so frightening and upsetting as you come to the blocking hedges, but, as you become accustomed to the layout and the flowers placed as clues, it is a wonderful game."

Mr. Bennet said, drily, "When I arise tomorrow morn, I shall pull my boots on and be right off for the chase. How about you, Reverend, is it not enthralling? We cannot leave for home without giving it a try."

"I shall not need directions from above. It is a spatial and mechanical game with a few geometric angles and very small widths on the ground to use as clues."

The group looked at him with bewilderment and were impressed with his grasp of the intricacy of the game.

The Reverend was not above fibbing to sound intelligent, and he had pretended the knowledge.

Charlotte was at her post by the window with the megaphone and Mrs. Bennet and Collins were blindfolded and led to the en - trances. They started out independently with laughter and teasing and then the heavy and concentrated search for the exit began.

Lizzy had offered her high brown shoes to her mother in the event the course was muddy, but she would not forsake her satin slippers and in about twelve minutes, she finished the game without a mud stain and was welcomed to the end with clapping and congratulations from the group upstairs as she had needed no shouted directions. She jumped up and down in delight, and joined Charlotte at the third story window.

"Just wait, my husband has a very poor sense of direction and he shall be down there for hours, never asking for help to free him."

Mrs. Bennet said, "I shall tell you my secret for speed. I just relied on my "Woman's Intuition".

"Thank God, but it is fine to have that pest occupied and out of the way. It is a bonus" thought Mr. Bennet, "I shall take some lunch and tea to Charlotte. She shall be up there all afternoon waiting for him."

This game was becoming unpleasant for her. Collins had spells of labyrinthitis and she scolded herself for forgetting to remind him as he ran off to the maze, but then, she knew all too well, that he would not own up to his handicap in front of the others.

She watched him down there, teetering and weaving about and had an inspiration. She invented a story and asked William to help to save Collins' face.

"Could you, please, say something like this? Tell the others he arrived at a spot that the gardener had made a mistake, and from that place, it was quite impossible to find a way out."

The audience had become bored and drifted off to dinner and then upstairs to nap, while the Darcys went about to rescue the Reverend.

It had been a perilous experience for him and he was tucked in bed for the day, his ears ringing and buzzing loudly and whenever he stood up he felt dizzy. He refused the offer of smelling salts and said he wanted to catch up on his Bible reading.

The next day, with the ladies sunning themselves in the gardens and William off to the butcher with a note from the cook, he tired of composing sermons in his head and set out for a hike around the grounds.

Collins had an actual physical need to talk and have listeners. There are people just born that way and even though they are loudly interrupted and told to keep still, they very rarely change. There are the others who say next to nothing and exhaust people who feel it is their mission to "draw them out." They make up a good size army of listeners.

The talkatives sometimes gravitate to the occupation of church minister and have a perfect outlet for their theories and unwanted advice. They adore their position behind the lectern on the church's altar where they can enjoy the sea of upturned faces and later point out which members they put to sleep with their sermons.

Rev. Collins decided to head to the back of the manor to talk to the gardener and his collection of young women who helped him pull out weeds and plant seeds.

"I have much experience in the art of gardening and I feel that I can bring up points that will enable you to have much more beautiful flowers and succulent vegetables than I see here now."

The gardener stopped what he was doing and listened, politely,

"First, and not least of all, it shocks me to see women other than gentlewomen, walking about in the garden choosing flowers for a bouquet. You must employ men-they are more appropriate to this form of manual labor. I think I will have a talk with Mr. Darcy about this. He is a man with a genial disposition and knowledge of the proper etiquette in running an estate like Pemberley."

The gardener, Mr. Harris, thought to himself, "Who is this nut and what business does he have, giving directions?"

"Excuse me, sir, I wish to point out that some of these women are my daughters and the rest are friends and cousins. They love the sun and fresh air and working with growing flowers, this is almost the only way they can earn money and, in another way, it would be cooking in a hot kitchen for them. I have hundreds applying for these jobs.

Here you are, I have a rose for you to put in your buttonhole. It is a rare hybrid and you shall be able to smell it's fragrance all day." (what a diplomat!)

Collins was disappointed with the gardener's quick dismissal and after a further stroll, he ran into Darcy's gamesman.

"I wish to speak with you about the gross distruction of wild animals and birds for sport at Pemberley."

"Ah dont know what ya mean, guvenah, the mastah keeps me in rifles and bullets so ah can help em shoot partridges for dinhah. Ah go with tha hunts and tha horses to catch foxes too. We dont eat foxes here, thats just fah a game, ah guess. Ah dont want to be with the huntahs, now ya explained it to me."

"Yes, my good man, it is an ethical and philosophical guestion and I have never been agreed with so readily.

I congratulate you on your understanding.

Can you now, direct me to the kitchen?"

Collins heard much laughter and loud conversation coming from the kitchen and was surprized to find Charlotte, Mary and Kitty perched on high stools drinking tea with the servants.

"My dear young ladies," he cried "You are keeping Mr. Darcy's employees from their work and I would wager Mrs. Reynolds' assistant cook wishes you away and out from underfoot."

"Dear Mr. Collins", his wife, Charlotte, answered, "Did you not hear the invitation from Mrs. Birdslap, our cook, after her delicious breakfast? We have been telling her over and over how much we enjoy her savory meals and she lives to hear these compliments, which are so well deserved. She has just now told me the directions for some of her best loved entrees, and how to find rare spices, as well. Some cooks keep their expertise secret. I can hardly wait to make something special for you."

"Well, I am happy to witness such favor and accord but I feel I must tell you that having crowds of people in the food preparation area is very unhygienic. There is too much breathing here and with each exhaled breath, there will be contamination. I know whole families at large state dinners can contract food poisoning from food prepared by cooks who deserved to be quarantined and sent to bed without pay. Mrs. Birdslap, did I not hear you sniffling and coughing as you served dinner last night? I think my only recourse is to talk with Mr. Darcy about you."

When Collins met Darcy, he had just been told by his games-keeper that he was quitting.

"He could not remember your exact words, but you made him feel like a murderer of animals and birds. Is that correct?"

"No, no, your gamesman is exaggerating. Please forgive me, I promise to keep away from your servants. They are a well chosen group."

The damage had been done before Darcy had the talk with him and he was to expect a visit from the gardener and the cook. Mrs. Birdslap was sobbing and wiping away tears with her apron. (Oh dear, more contamination.)

Mr. Greencastle wanted to be loud and clear about how he kept the grounds and the gardens of Pemberley and how they had always been kept for over one hundred years and if Mr. Darcy did not want women working in the gardens, he would have to fire his daughters and their cousins and their friends and when that happened, he and his crew would move to another estate to work and if that became the case, would Mr. Darcy kindly give him a letter of recommendation?"

William and Elizabeth were sitting together by the parlor window and saw Mrs. Birdslap coming from the outside wailing and blotting her tears. "Mr. Darcy, Sir, I want that man, Collins, kept out of my kitchen. He said the servants and the sisters and the guests are breathing out terible germs in the kitchen that will cause food poisoning and the deaths of everyone in the house. I think I shall have to ask Queen Alexandra for employment at Buckingham Palace. I have a standing offer from her."

Next came Rev. Collins again, weaving and dancing about as he did when agitated and knew he was going to be in Deep Trouble.

"Mr. Collins, my good fellow, I cannot have half of my servants unhappy and wanting to quit their jobs. I cannot conduct life in this house if I have to locate more servants to fill positions. I cannot have you strolling about criticizing and scolding my people who have always done admirable work and are like family to us. I trust you understand my position."

"Of course, I shall speak no more to your servants. I shall sit in my bedroom and read my Bible to find verses that will make me feel penitent. I spoke to your people because I felt they were breaking the Lord's commandments and His words in the Sermon on the Mount and they do not consider the letters written by St. Paul when he was locked in prison and also St. Francis of Assissi who guarded the animals and we must not forget the fine animals chosen to sail on Noah's ark and Christ feeding the multitudes at the seashore with fishes and loaves of bread."

Darcy wondered if this man was actually insane, as he suspected when meeting him the first time. He questioned Mr. Bennet, and he replied that Collins was way past insanity and suggested he skirt around him until an appropriate Madhouse could be found.

Collins continued, "I do hope you will understand the mode of my chosen profession and it's need for constant vigilance. I shall retire to my room for the rest of my visit, even forsaking the companion ship of my lovely wife. Kindly have my meals sent to my doorstep."

William and Lizzy fell into each other's arms, shaking with glee.

"Darling, there are some very silly people in my family, thank you for being patient."

"Lizzy, sweetheart, if that will keep the man in his room for the rest of the week, this will all be worthwhile and if I have to listen to the story of his rich sponsor, Lady de Bourgh and how he worships her, once more, I am heading for London. I have to say, though, that her wan and sickly little daughter, Anne has turned out well and, I just learned, is expecting. I hope we have a brief rest now."

Someone was alighting from a carriage by the portico- they heard the horse's bells- and saw with wonderment, that it was the Bennet's youngest daughter, Lydia, now Mrs. George Wickham. She had eloped with William's disliked foster brother and was the first Bennet daughter to marry.

"NO! NO!, please God do not let us see Wickham in the carriage with her. Here it comes Lizzy, we are still not free of our black sheep!"

Lydia had not been invited but she knew she would be welcome. Her Mother and sisters surrounded her with hugs and kisses and gathered up her luggage to go in for lunch. She said her husband was on a brief vacation from his brigade to go off to Brighton with his friends, and upon hearing that marvelous news, William gave a loud sigh of contentment.

"Lydie, sweetest darling girl, you must tell us All! How are you faring? You could write more often to your poor Mama and Papa. I see now, Lydie, are you not plump? Does she not look as if she is expecting, girls?" With that, she hit the nail right on the head.

Chapter Seventeen

Georgianna and Kitty had become cosmopolitan young women with their traveling and theatergoing and European friends and they were merry flirts with sure self confidence. There were few situations they felt they could not master, other than Georgie and Alex's complicated and unstable relationships and that could not be dignified by the word, romance, it. was more like a festering sore.

At least Kitty felt serene and in love. She was concentrating on her violinest Prince. Kitty was born with compassion for the sick and a delight with titles.

There was a restful period when Alex and Pierre were overseas and the girls liked to cool off in a pond on the road between the village and home. They told no one where they were swimming-William forbade it, strongly. There was a pretty lake by Pemberley but they loved a pond that had a waterfall and a big rock for diving. George Wickham, a man who had been raised with her almost as a brother when his parents died, would take Georgie, as a child, to that very pond, quite hidden from the road. She felt nostalgic. It was there she learned to swim.

Scheming about a swim in a forbidden pond was a giant step for Georgie, and Kitty loved to see these changes in her dear friend's personality. (One might say, she was a dangerous spirit.)

The girls walked to the village three days a week and they had the Pemberley carriage drive to the gate and wait there while they "walked and admired the scenery, on the way to the village."

The grounds of Pemberley were a mile or so in a forest where deer grazed comfortably with no fear of gun shots and when they returned, they found the driver in a slump and a good nap. Kitty took a branch to tickle him awake. He knew they were up to something because they returned wearing soggy clothes, but as a servant, he remained aloof and never commented on anything more than the weather. He did not want their fun to cease, if Mr. Darcy found out. The master would be all for a family picnic and a swim but he would be beside himself if he discovered the girls swam in the waterfall pond with only their camisoles and pantaloons as swim suits and Alone.

After diving and clearing a few rocks away from the pond bottom, they sat in the sun until their under clothes dried, but not too long or their suntans would emphasize their camisole marks and the upstairs maids would gossip.

"So, here we sit, at an impasse. Our families want husbands for us and grandbabies for them. Look at Anne, she is in perfect health and pregnant, looking prettier every day and just imagine the wealth and the estate she will inherit!"

With that, there was a clamor of breaking branches and Kitty was so startled, she fell back in the water. Two men, gypsies, ran down the path and one picked up Georgie and threw her face to the ground as he tied her legs and arms. She screamed and that brought out a bandana to go through her mouth and tie behind her head to muffle her cries.

Kitty tried to stay under water but the other man waded through the pond and caught her arm to drag her next to Georgie and tie-gagged her the same way. The men were rough and swift and the girls fainted.

"Don't use any water to wake them", Simon yelled, "They're easier to carry knocked out!"

Their carriage driver sat up front waiting to whip the horses forward while Simon and Judas pulled the girls to the back, holding them fast across their legs.

"Think of the money we'll get for these beauties. That brother of theirs has a fortune- have ya seen that castle they live in?"

They leaned forward on their seats and the girls began to moan as they realized they were stolen and Georgie recognized Simon as the man who had sidled up to her in the village and asked if she lived at Pemberley.

The drive was tortuous but mercifully short and they saw they had arrived in a forest clearing with long caravans used for sleeping, placed in a circle.

"Oh my", Georgie thought, "It is like pictures in a Fairy Tale book.

Simon dragged them from the carriage and Judas yelled, "Be gentle, you idiot! We get more money if they look good."

A pile of ragged quilts was waiting for them and an old white haired crone advanced from the onlookers to slash their bonds with a rusty knife. She smiled a toothless gesture and warned them not to try an escape because there were no houses nearby and they would be caught.

Georgie vomited and they shook with the cold and terror.

Gertie, one of the tribe, wiped them gently with a damp cloth and yelled at the men to get over there.

"I need four men ta carry them ta beds. They have no warm clothes on, ya don want em to catch pneumonia before ya get that ransom note out ta Darcy, do ya?"

The girls fancied being tucked into warm beds with sheets and warm quilts and were surprised to find themselves dumped on a pile of rags instead, beside a fire. Gertie was stirring something in a large cauldron that smelled good. They rubbed their arms and legs with bloody fingers and Kitty moaned, "I am dying" over a and over.

Georgie moved closer and said, softly, "William will pay them any ransom they ask for, just try to relax and warm up."

"He and Lizzy shall be so angry with us. They warned us not to swim there. Mama and papa shall be furious and never speak to me again, but I shall be dead anyway, so I will not care."

Gertie had sent for a young boy and he came to wait for instructions.

"As soon as it's dark, ya an Judas get on ya horses and ride ta town. They always have clothes left on their garden laundry lines. Get all ya can carry- pants and shirts, mainly.

Whats ya names, girlies? I'm Gertie. Ya'll be treated fine here tha men know ya can't be gave back all scraped an starving ta Mr. Darcy, they'd face a firin line. Mila an me always take care of tha camp's sick- she's ma daughta. Did ya see tha young lad? Ain't he a fine lookin one? He's ma grandson."

A question lingered with Georgie. "Since I have been kidnapped by a family of gypsy thieves who made bloody gashes and welts on my arms and face, am I obliged to admire a grandchild?"

Mila came through the open tent flap and was introduced. This was a camp of thieves and murderers but they had some manners.

"Oh, look at ya, ya needs a good wash. Ah'll get ma bucket of water and give ya a good scrub." She had left her pail in the sunshine and she had some clean looking rags, and at that point, any humble ministrations would seem nothing short of motherly.

Gertie said, "We always let a few days pass before we send the ransom note so we can get more money, so prepare yaselves for a wait. The men like to have their firecracker show when it's dark. ya all see, we have our fun here by tha fire."

Kitty leaned over and said, "I wonder how they would like to watch me dance a minuet and, Georgie, we could sing some Christmas Carols."

A cup of soup and bread crusts were offered and the girls dozed after dark as Simon came in with the boy and threw some clothes at them. They were too tired to do anything but pull them on and fall asleep.

Chapter Eighteen

There was a frightful scene at Pemberley, and a term of grief. William and Elizabeth were driven to the gate after a tiring trip from London. It was beginning to get dark and they were surprised to find Felix, one of their carriage drivers, sitting alone in their landau.

"Oh Master, oh Mistress, the young ladies took a walk to town at ten in the morning. I always wait here for them and I haven't seen them since they walked off!"

"Oh, my God!", shouted William, "Lizzy, get back in the carriage with me. We have to go back on the road to town to look for their things." There was a full moon and the driver lit some torches so they could make their way as they drove slowly back and forth. William took one side on foot and Lizzy, the other, stopping to crawl through the brush if they were attracted by something light or colorful by the side.

"William! Come here, I see a body." As they reached it they saw it was a dead fawn.

"If I find one of them in that condition, I shall go mad."

Felix knew he had to give the Darcys some information that could land him in terrible trouble and make him lose his job.

"Sir, the young ladies go somewhere to swim. I can tell because their clothes are askew and their hairdos are mussed when they come back to the gate. I don't think it's my place to ask questions so I just wait and drive them back to the manor."

"Great God, man! Are you crazy? Why did you not tell me that when we arrived? Here we have been driving up and down the road. Could you not have given us more information about the pond and directions?

"Wait, Lizzy, I have to contact the messenger, - no, come with me." They made another pass to town and with their new information, they knew where to stop and search. William had taken many swims by the waterfall and as they came near, they heard a loud splashing.

Each of them carried a lantern and climbed down to the pond. They found Kitty's and Georgie's dresses and shoes arranged neatly on the shore and shared an impulse to call their names over and over. They heard only the wind in answer.

"Quick, Lizzy, get back in the carriage, we have to wake the messenger." (the messenger was accustomed to being awakened for emergencies.) He took a hand written note by William and addressed to Calvin Strand, lawyer and detective. Although he had never dreamed he would need him, he had his name and address stored in his ·memory.

"Please find your way to this address in London as fast as you can, there will be a large sum of money for you."

The Darcys made their way slowly back to their house. Lizzy sobbed and William sighed over and over and cried with remorse. They faced the loss of two beloved sisters and they thought of the possibility of being called to identify two young women at a morgue or looking into fresh dug graves somewhere in the countryside.

Mrs. Reynolds met them at the door, offering food and loving concern on the dreadful night, but no kind words and hugs would lift a burden like a hammer pounding them.

William recognized an awful pain in his heart. He had the same soreness when each of his parents died and he was reminded of the very accurate description of the feeling that seems to come only with grief and a love that is spurned. A broken heart.

They sat together on the couch and William cradled and rocked Lizzy in his arms. He could not seem to stop saying, "It's my fault, it's all my fault." "William, it is not your fault, be kinder to your self, darling."

"But I did not do enough with the police when that knife was left with the flowers. And the fire crackers, oh, my God, it really is my fault. I did not warn them enough about the danger they could find on the road."

"William, come on now, they treated you as if they thought you were being a pest. Both of them could be saucy and independent. I often felt annoyed with them when they acted impatient. I should have cautioned them too. If it is anyone's fault, it is mine. Georgie told me a man came up to her in town and asked if she lived at Pemberley. I told her not to tell you- it would upset you. I am so stupid!"

"But Lizzy, Father made me Georgianna's guardian. I always tried to act more like her father than her brother. (Lizzy noticed, with sadness, that they were speaking of the girls in the past tense.) I am either too strict or too indulgent with her. I love her so. She is all I have left of my parents and our old life. She is my little sis, everytime I look at her I want to smooth her curls in place or brush off her jacket." He smiled for a minute. "I thought she might sock me one time when she was sixteen and I told her to tie her shoelaces tighter.

How can I know how to make little sisters happy? I bought her the piano, gladly, and she seemed to like the way I had her rooms decorated. It was simply not enough. She does not act all happy and light hearted like Kitty. I think you are right, she does need a husband and a home of her own. Do you think Alex Wright would be good for her? He acts wild about her but then, again, he is a tense sort of a guy. He acts bossy with her. Do women like that?"

"Sometimes, yes, and I often think there is a great excitement between them. She told me he does not approve of rich young women." "Oh, that won't do- he does not understand her. We shall have to double our efforts to find the right man. If we ever have her here again."

As often happens, when a loved person is lost or dies, their best traits are all that are remembered, and they become, as in the memory of Georgie, the most angelic of angels.

Mrs. Reynolds came to them with a pot of tea and scones and this time she was not easily discouraged. The Darcys ate and drank ravenously.

As some nourishment settled in his stomach and the tea cleared his mind, William said "Lizzy, I can see it all plainly now, the girls have been captured by the gypsies who have camped down on the west side of town. They know everyone in England who has great wealth. It is really surprising they have not struck me down before this. I guess they have been waiting patiently for us to have someone kidnapable living at Pemberley.

Come, Elizabeth, Let us get into bed while we are waiting for Detective Strand. We need rest so we are strong when he comes and tells us what to do."

There was no refreshing sleep at Pemberley.

121

Chapter Nineteen

The sisters, dressed like ragamuffins in mens' trousers and oversize shirts, barefoot and shivering, walked up the wide staircase to William's and Lizzy's bedroom. They felt numb with tiredness and could do nothing but gasp for breath and walk slowly to the foot of the bed.

William shouted, "Georgie!," and Lizzy screamed "Kitty!" They jumped from bed and made a place for each girl, tucking covers to their chins and placing hands on their brows to check for fevers.

"Simon and Judas drove us home. Gertie told us they heard you were hiring Detective Strand and if they were caught- it would mean their deaths. They left with us after they packed the tents and their things to run from town. Mira said, we were the nicest girls they had ever kidnapped. I kept thinking of my tombstone- "Here lies Georgianna Darcy, beloved by British Gypsies."

"I love you my dearest brother and sister! Kitty was crying, but managed to say, "Please do not be angry with us, we will never disobey you again."

Georgie continued, "As soon as they dropped us at Gertie's tent, they were nice enough and helpful and the sores on our arms and legs from the rope, felt much better after Mira put some stingy medicine on them."

Kitty got up from bed and said, "I do not want to disturb Mrs. Reynolds, but I must have some tea." Then she fainted and in slipping to the floor, hit her head on the night table. This was the site of a large black bruise for many weeks to come.

This episode, though with a happy ending, left the Darcys in a weak and painful state and they were annoyed to hear a loud knock, over and over, that took William to the front door.

Dawn was breaking and a huge man stood framed by the doorway and he had to stoop to get in.

"Detective Strand, Sir, Calvin Strand."

"Oh, come in, my good man, with all that has happened here tonight, I forgot that I sent the messenger to find you. Please let me have your coat. Did my stable boy take your horse? We have had a dreadful occasion here that has, thanks to God, turned out well enough.

Our sisters were abducted on the Derbyshire road, pulled undressed, and tied up in a carriage to take to a gypsy camp. I do not know how this information was found by the gypsies, but they heard that I had summonded you for help to recover the girls. They had planned a few days with them before sending the ransom note, but when they learned you were coming, they packed the entire camp and the girls were driven back here.

I think you must have a very worthy and wide spread reputation, and I would wager that you would have found Georgianna and Kitty, if they were still lost."

"Thank you for the kind words, Mr. Darcy, I shall now need a sound rest in bed. We shall discuss the matter after I have slept."

After a few hours, they heard him stirring and Mrs. Reynolds brought him a wonderful breakfast and tea. In truth, she brought him a second and third because he tore into the food as if he had not eaten in a week.

"Imagine if he lived here", she thought, "Land's sake he would go through a week's groceries in a day. He is twice the size of anyone human and I would need a kitchenful of extra workers to take care of his appetite." She shuddered as he complimented her and said he needed a cook and housekeeper at his flat in London and would she consider the job.? She was overwhelmed with all his good cheer but she had served the Darcys for over thirty years and she liked living in the country.

The girls were resting on sofas in the parlor propped with pillows and they had fresh bandages on their cuts Lizzy was playing the piano to amuse them and Kitty objected to her choice of music.

"Lizzy, please play something tuneful and lively, not Mary's kind of music, she plays sonatas that sound like funeral dirges. When we were at the gypsy camp, Judas played the violin and another was very good on the flute and the children were dancing in circles. It was a jolly scene."

"Oh, Kitty, how can you say anything nice about the gypsies when they tortured you in the carriage and stood ready to murder you if they received no ransom? Do not say anything more about liking these people. You cannot know how this has affected William. He spoke of leaving Pemberley so you would be safer and you know how he loves this home."

"Oh here you are, Mr. Strand, may I present our sisters, Georgianna Darcy and Katherine Bennet? Mrs. Reynolds went off to find William.

"Well, young ladies, you are very fortunate to be home again and so quickly, tell me the details of your adventure."

Kitty corrected him, "It was nothing as splendid as an Adventure."

"Katherine, take into account that Det. Strand has traveled over twenty miles on horseback, and at night, to come here to help us find you. Mr. Strand, please go on."

Georgie broke in with "I can show you where they tied us." She had sores around her mouth and she pulled up her sleeves to show the bloody welts on her arms."

"Yes, this is your typical kidnap. Sometimes they lay a blow to the victim's head to knock him out. I do not mean to make light of your experience, but if you had been hit with a lead pipe, you may never have regained conciousness."

"Oh, Mr. Darcy, the bed and breakfast were first rate. I am just having the young ladies' story- two very pretty damsels, I might add. You must have a doctor look over their wounds to determine the seriousness of their sores and if there is an infection- strong medicine is needed."

"I am not having any more stinging stuff on my arms. If anyone comes at me with cotton and needles, they will have to catch me."

"Katherine, remember our recent conversation? I want you to calm yourself and act respectful."

Kitty cried and sobbed at the scolding and Georgie wiped her tears with her silk dress, and said, "I am going to be a nun or I may stay in bed for the rest of my life."

No one was quite him or herself and Strand took over the proceedings.

He stood up and said "Now this is what we do in cases like this. I call in my policemen and they shall go through the town and the woods and give special attention to the site of the former gypsy camp. I am sure we have had trouble with this bunch before. I think so because they found out so soon that I was coming, and I recall the names, Simon and Judas. I do not expect much trouble. When we catch them, these young ladies can help us identify them.

Oh, Mrs. Reynolds, time for lunch? I have smelled a succulent stew brewing and you are not a minute too soon."

Det. Strand was realizing the happiest time of his life and having passed through the pretty town called Derbyshire, he already knew quite a lot about Pemberley. He was long widowed with no children and he wanted to set up a domicile in the countryside while he worked in London.

He had no friends in the area and he had dreamed of a plan to become acquainted with some of the pleasant townfolk. Since he was with the police, he was practised in strategies and directing operations. This may sound like too big an encompassing scheme for a rather simple need to win friends, but he was a big man and always did things in a big, or one might say, huge way.

(Readers, before I become lost in Detective Strands' Life Plan, I have to let you in on another scheme, this one generating in the kitchen at Pemberley. Just a hint, because guessing is fun.

Mrs. Reynolds had a brainstorm, and it had to do with Tilly the upstairs maid and a need for her to eat cake. There!)

Calvin Strand attended several hours of worship each Sunday at the Derbyshire Catholic Church and he felt more than welcome since the kidnap because the girls took him to the service and introduced him to the minister and their friends.

He was not a person to forget easily, and with his extreme voice, he filled a need in the choir. Basso Profundo.

The choir master was charmed to hear him sing in the front pew, and invited him to join the choir with his deep voice and commanding presence.

Kitty was enjoying her place beside him, he stood out so, and she had a new bonnet and a dress with short sleeves that showed off her bandaged arms and made her seem appealingly wounded.

The minister of a church in London told Det. Strand, frankly, that he should tone down his behavior and speach to become more socially attractive.

He was boistrous and clumsy and though he was a brilliant detective, his manner was, to some people, overstated. But, he had a horse and a devoted dog and they were his family. He was not exactly sad about having only animals to talk to but he felt at his age of sixty two, he needed a few people around him and being very rich, he could set up a wonderful country home. His horse, Figaro, knew he was an outstanding animal because he caused an excited commotion whenever he traveled with Det. Strand on his back and earned the largest and preferred stall wherever he was stabled. One could say that he was an engaging and theatrical horse and he had, in fact, been a circus attraction.

Strand saw him with great excitement at one of his performances and offered so much money to buy him, the circus owners bought a small town house in London. Figaro was the kind of horse called "Steely Muscled" and he carried his tall master perfectly. They were a popular pair and it would be easily believed that many damsels, through the years had begged for introductions- especially tall damsels. He preferred good cooks before beautiful women and a certain chemistry would roll through him when he smelled fine food cooking. It caused a delightful explosion of his senses.

Beef, freshly caught fish, carrots broiled in syrup and cakes baked with chocolate and almonds led him to peaks of gastronomic ecstacy.

It had been a long uncomfortable ride from London and when he was greeted by Mrs. Reynolds in an attractive night coat and carrying buttered scones and marmalade of her own recipe, his tired and weakened state made him fall instantly in love with her.

This was a day more delightful than any in his experience, that gave him the acquaintance of the gracious and very elegant Darcys, their adorable and friendly sisters, and mainly the introduction to Mrs. Reynolds and her rich kitchen fare.

After mapping and explaining his next visit with the police in attendance, he asked the Darcys if he might stop in for lunch or dinner whenever he was near Pemberley. He insisted he would take no payment for guiding the case, he wanted only the promise of short visits and delicious meals.

Could there be any less to do for this friendly man who had ridden many miles through the night to help them find their sisters? Amazingly, the unusual "Payment", began immediately. Det. Strand was not one to let grass grow between his toes.

He headed for the kitchen to find Mrs. Reynolds but the downstairs maid told him she was in the laundry room folding sheets and pointed to a room next door.

He bumped his head upon entering the laundry but this did not daunt him. He had a permanent black and blue bruise on his forehead from colliding with door jams.

"Mrs. Reynolds, you have outdone yourself, never have I tasted a more savory stew with pickled Madagaster corn and not the least, your dessert triumph, lemon and lime feffernussen. Have I heard correctly that these recipies are of your invention? Mrs. Reynolds, I wish to be frank with you, God did not intend you to fold sheets and press curtains, you deserve a life of culinary fame devoted to cooking in the finest kitchens, some place like the kitchen of our King and Queen, or at my country home, which I will build to your specifications, in Derbyshire when you decide to be my cook. You will do no housekeeping, you will have servants of your own. Mrs. Reynolds, I beg you to tell me when I can expect you."

Mrs. Reynolds had been studying Strand since he arrived and thought he was so much fun, but he was like a circus freak with his enormous height and his giant horse.

If she worked for him, she would never have to stand on wobbly chairs or ladders to reach things, he would be right beside her helping, as he was then. She had been a widow for thirty years and had never received so much attention from a man. It was an exciting novelty for her. She decided immediately that she didn't want to live with him and work in his kitchen, even if it would be designed for her, and was annoyed at his manner of sabotaging the Darcys. She did, however, accept his offer of a short stroll in the garden and thought this would slow him down, but instead, he was sure he was gaining ground.

After sleeping on the matter, she devised a plan. If she was going to have to put up with his constant hovering and the good possibility that she would have to feed a corps of London policemen, she was going to demand a treat of her own.

Her idea of a treat was a horse to stable with the Darcys' and William and Lizzy said she deserved a horse and surely, all the arrangements could be started the very next week. They realized that Det. Strand was ready to compete heavily for her services, and possibly her heart.

William remarked to Elizabeth, "You know how we strive to respect our servants but this is getting out of hand."

Chapter Twenty

During the week of the kidnap, and knowing nothing of the horrendous events in the Darcys' lives, Alex felt a longing for Georgianna and a thrilling inspiration came to him.

He would drive to Derbyshire and attend Sunday's service at the Catholic Church. He felt confident the Darcy family would be there. This plan was more appropriate than appearing uninvited at Pemberley and he felt eager as he dressed in his new suit and high lizard boots.

As he waited in his carriage under a concealing maple tree, he saw the girls arrive with an enormous man.

"What on earth? Is one of them engaged to that giant?"

He could never guess who or what Det. Strand was, but he loved Georgie's surprised smile as she moved closer to the Detective to make a place for him and gave her hymnal so they could sing together.

During the offering, he leaned across her to give his hand to Strand and introduce himself and he smiled at Kitty who was puzzled.

"For Heaven's sake!" (His extended arm brushed her.) "That was rude and very familiar, but it felt so nice."

"Dear God, forgive these thoughts in your church, Alex is just here to flirt with me in his maddening, creative way."

The Priest read a verse from Psalms- "But let thee be kind and loving, sharing the gifts of the Holy Spirit." "She thought the Bible was often romantic and always a comfort.

"Now here is Alex and I will be weighted down with confusion and guilt, the way he always makes me feel. Why does he not stay at his farm and release me?"

Alex, instead, felt gloriously happy, sitting beside his passion, who, as usual, had the scent of blooming flowers. ("She must have given her dogs a good scrubbing.")

He was content to sit and listen to a lenghty sermon that was a warning to avoid the sins of the flesh. (So very appropriate.)

At last the service ended and as they gathered outside, he accepted Georgie's invitation to dinner and followed their carriage on the road to Pemberley.

The conversation at the Darcys' table astonished him. He had not heard of the kidnap and was frightened to know his darling had almost been snatched from him forever.

Later, as she walked with him to his carriage, he scolded

"Why did you not heed your brother's warning about swimming in the pond? You have caused William and Lizzy a great deal of worry and pain."

"Yes doctor, Kitty and I are well aware of all of that, why can you not simply say, "My darling Georgie, if you had been killed, I would have impaled myself with my dagger, or something Shakespearian like that?" She covered her mouth so he could not see she was laughing.

"Alex, you are hopeless, You cannot bring yourself to say anything close to I love you.

Goodbye, have a safe ride!" she called as she ran to the manor.

He called after her, "My flowers say I love you!", but she did not hear. In fact, his bill at the florist rivaled everything he spent for his profession.

....

William and Elizabeth sat together having tea and he remarked, "Here we thought our only project was to find husbands for our sisters, and, instead, we have a courting and romancing by a seven foot detective for our elderly cook. Please do not take offense, but since your sister came to live here, the atmosphere at Pemberley has become, shall we say, a study in mayhem."

....

The formerly "stolen by gypsies" Darcy and Bennet, had arrived at a somewhat tarnished acceptance and were no longer, if only temporarily, treasured young sisters. As usually happens, runaways and the kidnapped reach a point of discovering their families are angry with them after all the pain they have caused.

When the girls were rested and healthy, and there had been some conjecture about how often they could expect the Detective for lunch, William remarked that if he would have to deal with an overworked and tense cook's services on a once a week basis, they could either walk to town with Strand to keep him out of Mrs. Reynold's hair or wash laundry and pin it up to dry and, as an afterthought, he told them all of this calamity would not have occurred if they had obeyed him and he and Elizabeth thought they were acting like ten year olds.

This was the first time William had stepped into the role of stern father, and they listened nervously with heads bowed, playing with dress ribbons and buttons, and when their brother finished scolding, they raced to their bedroom.

As they lay in their beds, engulfed with comforting dog and cat friends, they reassessed their behavior and agreed they had to work on Maturity.

....

"Elizabeth, if I remember correctly, Your parents are stopping here on their way to visit the Gardiners. Such a shame with the timing. I wish they would not hear about the trouble and the kidnap-it would be hard on both of them, at their ages.

I cannot think of any way to notify them so they will not arrive when there are policemen, vans horses, and search dogs all over our pathways."

"Yes, my darling and thoughtful William, It would seem we have some hectic weeks ahead of us, but we trusted God to return our sisters and now He shall guide us through the coming days.

William do you know of anyone who has a Guardian Angel? I have a feeling, more and more, that a loving Spirit is caring for us.

Sweet dreams, sweetheart."

Chapter Twenty One

Fate danced right in and had it's way. The Bennets, Lizzy and Kitty's parents, arrived at Pemberley at exactly ten in the morning. There were eighteen horses and policemen and the carriages carried the message "Police Department of Southern England" posted on their sides and Mrs. Bennet screamed as their landau came to a stop.

"Oh, Mr. Bennet," she managed to ask from the carriage floor, "what have Lizzy and Kitty done?!" (It was apparent that these two daughters were not her favorites.)

The suspicion of some devilment by Kitty was, this time, right on. She had sent Kitty willingly and happily to live at Pemberley with the surest confidence, to learn ladylike and educated ways. Now she found herself in dreadful fear that Kitty had brought all of Pemberley and the Darcys down around her eighteen year old shoulders. Mrs. Bennet was known for her hysterical and pessimistic nature and she always pointed out the worst that could happen and then was happily relieved when nothing close to her fears developed.

Lizzy ran out the door to meet her parents. The Police rigs had scratchy horns and she heard one loud blast. "Mama! All is well here, we had some trouble but now we are fine. Papa, dearest, oh, it is sweet to see you both, did you have a comfortable drive? Mama, no, I do not have any smelling salts, just come over to the bench and we shall all sit quietly for awhile and I shall tell you what has happened."

William came along and kissed Mrs. Bennet and helped Lizzy fill in the story. He explained that the girls were in the kitchen beside Mrs Reynolds, preparing dinner for eighteen policemen, a detective and the six of them. He remarked that Elizabeth had often complimented him on his clairvoyance, or mental telepathy, or whatever it could be, and he was certain they would arrive at just this strange and most humorous of moments. At that point, the events still seemed humorous.

William excused himself and said he was about to drive to town to pick up some food- many pounds of food.

Mr. Bennet could not stop laughing. He reminded them they had sent Kitty to Pemberley to rid her of her silly ways and here she was, passing on her nonesense to lovely and dignified Georgianna Darcy.

"My stars!"

Mrs. Bennet had just caught sight of Detective Strand, all seven feet of him, riding from the gate on a monstrous horse.

"What is that person? Who is that person? Mr. Bennet, stop your laughing, you are rude!"

Lizzy made the introductions and Strand galloped off to the manor, calling that he had to help Mrs. Reynolds.

"We have a suitor here, mama, for our housekeeper's hand." "Oh, Lizzy tell me this is not true. This place feels almost thick with wildness, I suspect Kitty is guilty of the mischief. Do you still have a ghost in the attic?"

"No, no, Mary's fiancé came to perform a service to let him go. We have not heard from him since."

Mrs. Bennet came to realize that there was much happening at Pemberley that she might be happier not knowing.

"Now, let us go in to the kitchen to greet the hardworking Misses Darcy and Bennet."

The girls were aproned and perspiring heavily as they chopped vegetables. Mrs. Reynolds was very impatient and insisted that Detective Strand remove himself from the manor until dinner. No one had witnessed Her Anger in the thirty some years she had worked at Pemberley, and this noon she yelled, "Get out of here, Strand! I cannot come out now to chose a horse, are you crazy?! If you build a house near here, I shall move to London and never give you my address."

Metaphorically speaking, the girls' innocent swim in the pond was causing repercussions at Pemberley similar to an invasion of ravenous tigers.

Mr. Bennet enjoyed the scene. It was chaotic but far more entertaining than living at home and he had not laughed so hard in years.

A bad ache was developing over Kitty's forehead. Her mother wanted "a long talk with her" and since she was prone to migraines, now, seemed as good a time as any, to complain of one.

Det. Strand lorded over the dinner table as if he was the master of the house, and he praised the meal, even though it looked like peasants had thrown it together, but three chocolate cakes flavored with almonds renewed Mrs. Reynolds' reputation.

Some of the policemen asked for the recipe to give their wives and went out to take naps under the trees.

Mrs. Bennet took Kitty aside with a promise to keep her for only a minute as they started to dry dishes.

"Mama, please be gentle with me, I have such a sore head and I feel like sitting still for awhile."

"Kitty, I would not dream of hurting you, just come over and sit by me. "I want you to observe four of the policemen. The two dark haired ones with mustaches and the fair one with blue eyes, and the tall one. No, no, not Det. Strand."

They seem like pleasant and intelligent young men and all unmarried and well mannered. Now, since I think I remember correctly, they may be returning to hunt for gypsies, I want you to dress attractively and make yourself acquainted with them.

Georgianna can do your kitchen work. She will never have to search for a husband the way you do. She knows she will never have to cook and clean with a huge dowry like hers." (Mrs. Bennet had not heard that only a few weeks remained until Kitty announced that she was engaged to a Prince.)

"Oh, Mama, I can always count on you to be the same. All you can think of is getting me married even though a short time ago, I was kidnapped and barely escaped with my life. You may be right-perhaps a policeman would be the right husband for me, I am still getting into scrapes. I am too exhausted for all of this, I think I should go in now and help Georgie with the dishes. I am so glad to see you and Papa. I love you."

Chapter Twenty Two

The Darcys were planning an Ocean voyage to Savannah, Georgia to see his rice and cotton businesses, and decided to take a group of friends along. There was a necessity, by law, to have a doctor aboard and they had advertised in "The London Times" and interviewed a number of applicants and there were none that suited them. The date to sail was coming close.

Elizabeth was in the market and heard some very good news. One of the ladies, whom you might call gossips, had heard that Alex Wright, that attractive young doctor, was at his home office in Highlands, on leave from his missionary work in India.

Elizabeth asked William to beg him to come on the voyage. She had never been to America and wanted to see Savannah before she became pregnant. They expected Georgie to accompany them on the drive, as they were innocent of knowing his feelings for her but wanted her to get over the grudge she held against him.

On a beautiful morning, the kind of a day when Fate is at it's happiest, William knocked on the doctor's door, and when there was no answer, he was about to return to the carriage. Alex had watched them arrive and he saw Geogianna step down to give Rumpus some exercize. He was in his garden, shirtless, tying grape vines to a post.

"Oh dear God, now I have to see her and talk to her just when I was starting to forget her. It hadn't done much good to find a piece of her jacket, the one she wore to the dog show, under his examining table. He held it to his lips, this was probably the only thing he would ever have of her, except her cold notes. "Well, this is going to be a stiff test of my composure. I can not hide unless I fall to the ground. Damn it, where is my shirt?"

He looked tan and well muscled and glowing with the heat. "There is nothing for me to do except act pleased. "Look at her! She has grown a little taller and even more beautiful. Good God! Why do I need to be tortured like this? They will tell me she is engaged and a handsome fiance will step from the carriage."

Well, here it is. "Hello Darcys, what a good surprise. Did you know I am back from India for a few months? Mrs. Darcy,

139

Georgianna, he bowed, have you any news to tell me? I feel as if I have been gone for too long."

"No, not at this time, today, we have an invitation and an offer of a job", William said, "It would be a big help if you will come across the Atlantic with us to visit Savannah, Georgia. I have rice and cotton fields and I want to meet my partner. These young ladies and some of our friends will accompany us. It will be about a three months excursion with time to travel in the southern states. I do not expect you to give an answer immediately but we hope to set sail in two weeks."

Rumpus had caught sight of Alex's dog and they tore off through the fields. There was nothing for Georgianna and Alex to do but chase after them.

As soon as they were hidden by tall grass and fell down, out of breath, Alex said, "Georgianna, You are not in my Life Plan."

"That is silly of you.", Georgie panted, "No one knows the plan of our lives but God and He is the only one with the directions. I want to marry soon and I cannot marry you. Why on earth do you think I would want you for a husband? I just came along on the ride because it is a nice day. You are acting all complicated and difficult, as usual."

"There is nothing complicated about the fact that I do not want to marry you. You are not the only desirable woman in England, though you appear to think so."

"Fine. Your lack of interest delights me. I shall keep out of your way if you decide to come on the voyage. We have jolly friends who are sailing with us and there are balls planned for Kitty and I to meet some American men. You, most likely, have no formal suits and do not know how to dance. If you just decide to stop acting so intense and pouty, you might enjoy yourself."

She carried Rumpus back to the carriage and Alex followed "Mr. and Mrs. Darcy, I want to tell you now, I shall come on the voyage."

"Wonderful! Let us shake on it and meet again on Wednesday to discuss our plans. Shall you have some time to talk with me?"

The Darcys were relieved and excited to have the matter settled so pleasantly. Now it was full sail ahead!

Georgie found a pencil in her purse and wrote something before climbing in the carriage. She folded it and asked him to read it when they were gone.

"What a dunce I am! I shall lose her on this voyage if I decide to ask for her hand. Balls to meet American men! What chance have I? Fate steers me on dangerous courses. Dear God, help me!"

"The note, ah, the note, this will be sweet. A note in her own hand, as lovely as she is." It read, "I will break your heart one day." He read it over and over and then he burned it.

That night, after a day of worry and remorse, he could not sleep. His heart was pounding so, he thought he could hear it and he wished he would die. "Dear God and all the fates, why do you dangle that girl before me? I cannot have her, I do not want her, she looks adorable in that shade of blue, her eyes are the color of amethysts, and all that long, shining blonde hair, I want to take it down and brush it. I can just see her sitting there on my bed with that glorious hair swirling around her. She must be miserably spoiled, imagine her going on a sea voyage with all the luxuries and she is not yet twenty. How shall she do without servants? Take them along, no doubt. Her lips and cheeks are naturally rosy. I have seen that only in children, imagine what our children would be like, I could ask for nothing more than to have children that were little Georgiannas. She smiled and tilted her head as she stepped from the carriage. She has so many pretty mannerisms. She took my hand, I wanted to be alone so I could pull her to me. Thank Heaven they left soon enough. I did not even have a shirt on. I have nothing but bad manners."

Georgianna was in a happy mood on the ride home and sang church hymns to herself as she polished her nails with a kerchief. She knew she had Alex. She would decide on the voyage if she wanted him. She could not sleep that night. "What a nerve he had, acting as if I had come to Highlands just to tease him and make him want me. I would never do such a stupid thing, but I have to admit, it crossed my mind, back and forth, and back again. He is a common country doctor. Oh, what a tall, beautiful body he has. I adore his muscles and his wide shoulders and his strong upper arms. So this is what the authors of romance novels go on and on about. There can be no man as beautiful as Alex, he looks so powerful. I wanted to kiss his lips and hug him close to me." She was surprised that despite all the running and tackling dogs, he smelled wonderful.

If I married him, I would have to be a missionary. Imagine? I am sure India is beautiful, rich people travel there, we could be tourists, occasionally, and use my inheritance. I could have his precious children, to start, we will have two boys, the first to look just like him and the next will be like William. (Everyone tells me he is the handsomest man they have seen.) Then, our daughters shall look like Alex too and the whole bunch shall have curly, golden hair.

Oh, I should not want him. He is a nobody and he has country manners. Imagine coming to greet people without a shirt on?

I love his tanned, strong body. Oh, dear God, I am lost with foolish yearning! Whenever I close my eyes, he is standing before me. Why do I find it exciting when he scowls? I am, plainly, going crazy. At least he speaks well and has graduated from Universities. I must not think like this, I sound like a superior little nit. Kitty would laugh at me, she wants to marry a Prince and William would have a stroke, after all the complaining he does to Lizzy, saying he does not want me darning socks so I could be a good wife for a street cleaner or a missionary."

Chapter Twenty Three

"Fate is having the nastiest fun with us. Lady de Bourgh would laugh at me. No, perhaps not, after all, she allowed Anne to marry a blacksmith. If someone asked her, "Did you hear that Georgianna Darcy is marrying a missionary?, She would answer, "Yes, it seems to be the current vogue- wealthy girls marrying men with simple professions. I find it most pleasant."

I am such a snob. I criticize blacksmiths and country doctors. I do not deserve Alex, he can be so kind sometimes and he is handsome and wise."

The next morning, she waited impatiently for William and Lizzy to leave for London. She combed her hair to curl around her shoulders and as soon as they departed, she asked the stable boy to ready the small carriage.

He asked, "I don't mean to act cheeky, Miss, but does tha mast ah know ya are travelin with the carriage today? He did na say nathin afore he left. Is he forgetful?'

"I will be safe. I like to drive in the country on sunny day days."

The morning began with sunshine, but as she drove, she looked ahead to see dark storm clouds gathering. What could she do but continue to Alex's house, it was the closest.

It began to pour in blowing sheets of rain and lightning crackled through the trees. She hated thunderstorms and prayed for safety.

A much needed insight came to her. "I am a childish woman, causing trouble all around me, like a whirlwind." She was soaked and his home was a haven.

His housekeeper opened the door. "I am sorry, Miss, the doctor is with a patient. Please come in, you are soaked, you may sit by the fire, I shall find a towel for your hair."

She heard Alex talking to someone in his office. "I am glad you came by carriage, this is quite a storm but I think I see some blue skies up there." Then he walked into the parlor and looked bewildered.

"Look at me. I feel so silly, I am soaking wet."

"But why are you here?"

"Remember, I told you I would stay out of your way on the voyage? I have come to kiss you beforehand, and hug you and have you scold me. That is what you like to do best with me. This is your last time alone with me,"

He ushered her into the examining room and pulled her ribbon off to let her hair flow loose." Take off your wet clothes and put on this coat of mine. We will dry them by the fire, but it may take awhile. Call me when you are undressed and have your clothes to give to Mrs. Webster."

"This girl is wildly impetuous- I guess that is why she is so beguiling. I do not want her driving here alone. It is not safe. She said she just wants to kiss and hug me. I hoped we were all finished with that. Dear Father in Heaven, I can not keep pushing away all this temptation. Our relationship is like something Shakespeare would write. "Star crossed lovers", people like that. She and I seem to push each other away and then pull passionately together again.

Now I have lost all my concentration for my patients.

I shall have Mrs. Webster take her upstairs and put her under covers. She may get sick. What do I do now?"

"Do your brother and sister -in-law know you are here?" he called.

She did not hear him. "I could go up there and be in bed with her in two seconds. My patients could wait. This is one more test of my morals and character. I am exhausted with this assault."

Georgie was not sick, she was completely dry and bored. She wanted him to hold her and kiss her. Instead, she was left to consider ways to redecorate the room. "He has patients, of course, at age nineteen, I have come to realize that the world does not spin around for Georgie Darcy. What a silly self centered woman I am."

The storm was past and she called downstairs, "Mrs. Webster, I shall like my clothes now, I am going home."

"Here I sit, Alex is avoiding me and I do not know where he is. What a futile trip."

"The doctor went to the village for medicine, would you like some tea?"

"No, thank you, I shall be on my way."

"Now I know he is serious. He really does not want to marry me. Oh, I am so stupid, some one should lock me up to prevent me from doing things like this. I am so ashamed."

Alex returned just in time to miss her. He walked to the bed room and there was her scent. She had made the bed very neatly and there was a note on the cover.

"I still do not want to marry you. EVER."

He sighed. "This is all I have of her. A collection of rejections, this one hand delivered."

Chapter Twenty Four

The ship was ready and tied up at the dock in London. William was anxious to take some of his co- passengers to see it, all ready for the voyage. It was very grand and imposing, with masts and huge sails ready to billow with wind and take them to America.

Phillipe was in wonderment at this lucky opportunity to sail and told William he had crossed the Atlantic several times on smaller ships and Nettie and Anton agreed it was far superior. The twins nearly swooned and rambled on and on in French and English about their days on the Vaudeville Stage and their trips across the ocean to star in Mr. Carl's shows.

Lizzy tried to muster courage and pretended to be enthusiastic, but three weeks ahead on troubled waters- "Heavens, how I wish I were pregnant and did not have to go."

The girls stood back a bit and Georgie said, "I did not expect to feel frightened and I do not want to go, I wonder if the Gardiners would take us for an extended visit. What do you think, Kitty?"

"Frankly, I have such a headache I do not know what I think." Lizzy sensed their fear and suggested they think ahead to Savannah and the beautiful places they would see and the balls that were planned just for them and the possibility they would meet some men to marry.

No one had guessed that Kitty was in love with Philippe, despite his eccentricities, and had discovered she had a strong maternal streak. Just perfect for that Prince's Princess.

Georgie sat Kitty down beside her.

"You know what we are forgetting? Philippe will be with you and when he is not having one of his "Sick fits", he can be jolly. Nettie told me he was treated badly by his mother and that is why he is a touch neurotic. Why not devote the trip to giving him the right sort of attention and that way, you will be less concerned with your fears, if you are worried about the weather, he shall walk you around to distract you and make you laugh. When I first met him, I thought he was terribly attractive but much too strange for everyday friendship, but now that I have become better acquainted, I like him.

And for me, I shall dally with the doctor's affections. Keeping him in his place shall be more than enough games for me.

You know, Kitty, when I hear myself say things like that, I fear I am becoming a heartless witch.'"

Kitty laughed and said, "You are not heartless, but you can be witchy."

"Oh, well, one thing we must remember, at all cost is to pack trunks full of salt bisquits and tea bags. Jane Bingley told Lizzy she finally became a seasoned traveler with the wafers she took to overcome her morning sickness."

....

The Bingleys were at the dock to kiss and hug and say farewell to the hardy sailors. How they wished they could go. (There are things wives have to endure and Jane was faking) but their baby would soon be born and when another trip came up, they were the first to sign on.

Dr. Wright arrived early so he could not miss the chance to feel superior. The trunks! More and more were delivered to the hold. Apparently, these people could not survive with less than three changes of clothes per day! "I shall wear my black shirt and trousers and I have my black evening suit with the white ruffled shirt and satin vest."

Alex did not realize it but, in reviewing his wardrobe, he sounded like the aristocrats he criticized.

"Oh, no, there she is. I shall smile politely, nothing more. This voyage shall take raw courage and demanding restraint. Oh, Dear God, now she is coming over."

"Good morning, Dr. Wright,"

("It is a very formal greeting, but she warned she would stay from my path.")

He turned quickly to greet the Tremblants who were all aflutter, and said Hello to Kitty, who was hanging on Philippe's arm and claiming him as her own, and, at last his host and hostess. The Darcy's were friendly and likeable people, nothing like typical frosty aristocrats.

Pushing ahead were Nettie and Antony, also, seasoned travelers. Alex hoped they had packed cards and books. He had suffered seasickness and he was prepared to be compassionate.

All went well, away from home for a day. The twins had two trunks of costumes from their Vaudeville days, and they expected to wear a different outfit each evening and do a little dance and sing a few ditties. But at five o'clock there was A Crisis. The costumes were too tight and they went to work with scissors to open seams but it was to no avail, and they became panic strickened and saught advice from the doctor.

He prescribed a glass of wine apiece and they were soon off to Dreamland, where all their costumes fit.

The Darcys were strolling on the deck after dinner and admired the stars and planets. They had great hopes for the trip an and these were not vain wishes.

The next morning, Lizzy asked William to bring a pot or a pail, anything, and she felt seasick all day, William conferred with Alex and he went in to Lizzy to ask a few key questions. He asked her to do some counting back in the month.

"I do not wish to embarrass you, Mrs. Darcy, but I think you are pregnant." She jumped up and gave him a kiss and then fell back blissfully against the pillows and asked Alex to find William.

It was a time to celebrate! This was a good omen and they decided to to tell the news immediately and felt it would be a an auspicious trip.

The rest were falling into a routine of meals and cards and a new game, Charades.

Alex held the conviction that card games were vain and foolish, but each to his own, especially since they were playing for money. He had none and felt ill at ease and depressed.

"Where in the devil was Georgie?"

He walked slowly with his nose in a book, trying to look as if he was searching for no one and was pleasantly occupied.

'Ah, Hah! There she was, over by the captain. She was sewing and laughing, and the captain was a suntanned, handsome man of about fifty. When she saw Alex, she waved, he waved back.

Georgie planned to act like a coquette, that would annoy Alex, and she thought the captain was really quite fascinating.

She was having a good time.

Chapter Twenty Five

Soon after they were in full sail, Lizzy asked Alex to join her on a stroll around the deck and said, "I probably should not be saying this to interfere, but I have a feeling that you are in love with Georgianna. You remind me of William when I first knew him. He could barely give voice to his feelings. He would ride his horse from London to our house just to sit with me and all he could say was, "How are your parents? And your sisters? And your grand parents, are they also well? It is a fine summer day. And you, are you well too?"

He did not act like a University trained scholar, he acted like the village simpleton. When he finally proposed, he began by telling me that my family acted like common folk and they were well beneath him and pointed out that I was lucky that he wanted me for his wife.

He was the total opposite of his foster brother, George Wickham. George was known all over town as a cad, but I was so drawn by his charming ways. His disposition is so sunny but he has quite the reputation for casual seduction.

William and I like you and I am telling all of this to you because I see your mistakes with our sister. She told me that she would like to have a man who was a father and a lover to her. She likes older men who are sensitive and I can see her settling in at Rose Haven, playing her piano, designing her quilts and raising your children. (At that comment, Alex beamed.) As you know, her dowry is a vast fortune. You might use some of that money for "grace notes" in your marriage for weekends in London to attend the ballet and the opera and do a bit of world traveling.

Our musician friend, Philippe, has a good courtship style. The moment he sees Kitty in the morning, he gives her a little hug and kiss and says something like this, "Kitty, my precious darling little kitten, did you have sweet dreams? I could hardly sleep from wanting you. Let me take your arm and go out to the railing so I may cool myself." "Kitty loves all of this, she knows this is exaggeration, but he is such a nut and so much fun.

Now when you two met this morning, I overheard you say, "I hope you have kept your hands away from your wounds, I hate to see the way you keep touching. your shoulder, I want you to act grown up about this."

Have you not a sister or mother still alive? You do not seem comfortable with women. Georgie told me that you would not let her teach you to dance for the balls in Savannah. That is the life she knows, she has spent most of her life in a mansion the size of Buckingham Palace and she has servants to help her with her every need. That is the style of life she knows. She is a cultured young society woman. William has worked with her about the problems she has. He is her legal guardian and he takes that role very seriously. I think he has done a fine job with her, she is so sweet and unaffected and has good values. I just love her as a sister-in law.

If you let Georgianna slip through your fingers, you will regret it for the rest of your life.

In talking all this through Alex, I think if you do not take emergency steps to improve your manner, as a suitor, you are hopeless. William and I often talk about the two of you and wish that you could appreciate each other and be close."

With that, she was off to lunch.

Alex knew that every thing she said was true. Georgie acted sweet and giving and natural until he provoked her. She burned his flowers. That had probably never been done in the history of romance, and now he could laugh about it- and he thought she was creative and spirited. If she did not, care for him at all, she would have said, "Oh, Mrs. Reynolds, would you please, find a vase for these, I shall write a thank you note when I am not so busy."

How he wished he had the manners of Darcy and that Col. Fitz William who runs their business. "He is a man of good looks and refinement and wealth. I suspect he has proposed to her and she is to decide if she likes Savannah well enough to live there."

He knelt down to pray. "Dear Lord, if I can make her happy, I want Georgianna for my wife." He knew it was wrong to bargain in prayers but he was so hungry for her he did not know what he was doing. "I shall give my life to you and be your missionary."

In his heart, he knew more than prayers were needed at that point.

He went back to his cabin and sat holding his pen. He could be methodical and he decided to think of compliments to tell her and write them down. He had noticed that the aristocrats used endearments when they talked to each other.

He decided to start with a heading.

"On this day in 1882, Alexander Wright composed these loving sentiments to win the hand of Georgianna Darcy". With each word, he prayed that she would be his.

"That was a start with a flourish," he thought. Through the afternoon, nothing came to his mind. He had a paralyzing writer's block. He had never had a need to express his feelings. After three hours, he was about to ask the Prince to help him but then, a good idea came to his mind. He retrieved a bottle of wine from his shelf and after downing three glassfuls, he felt as poetic as Robert Browning.

Compliments-

Number One - Georgie, sweetness, you look well rested and bright this morning.

Two - Please sit beside me at dinner. You always smell like bouquets of roses. "Oh no, that would remind her of the flowers of mine that she burned."

Three - Georgie, my little daisy! You have a wonderful perfume! I suspect that your flowery scent is just natural to you,

Four - How is your stomach? Oh, That is bad.- I hope you have no sea sickness on the trip, precious. Let us walk around the deck and watch the sea. I can think of no one else that I would rather stroll with.

Five- Has your brother had your portrait painted? An artist should capture your looks at just this age. (He thought that was the best, so far.)

Six- Will it be alright if I tap my shoulder to remind you not to upset your wound? Sometimes I feel you need a loving father's care.

Seven-You are the most beautiful woman I have seen. I think God sent your funny Rumpus to bring you to me at the show.

(He had read somewhere that beautiful women are used to hearing they are lovely so to make a really splendid impression, one should compliment them on something about them that is not so apparent.)

Eight-Elizabeth told me you are so good with languages and you are a very bright young woman, and an artist as well.

....

He felt so fired up, he went to the first deck to find her and she was sitting next to William and sewing a large cover. He greeted them and sat down.

William was acting petulant. "Georgianna, why do you persist in sewing these covers of patches?" He knew why but he was in a bad mood and wanted to bring it up again. "Where do you find these raggy patches? There is no one at Pemberley dressed in rags, my servants have new uniforms, they eat well too. The dogs and cats have expensive collars and are well fed, The whole lot of them are well dressed and healthy."

"William, I buy my scraps from the rag mongers cart. You know that my quilts are a form of art. Lizzy tells you that over and over. You are so tiresome sometimes and you are embarrassing me before the doctor."

"I am sorry, darling sister, I shall take myself somewhere to have a glass of wine. Adieu."

"Show me your quilt, Georgie, is this all your design or do you follow a pattern? Let me stretch it out so I may have a better look. Honestly, this is really beautiful. I have never seen anything like it."

Georgie sensed something new brewing and decided to keep sewing and smile occasionally.

"I hope you will not take this in the wrong way, but..."

"Well, here comes his usual scolding," Georgie thought. "I notice you are sensitive in your wound area. Is it aching and itchy? Ask the cook to give you some ice and wrap it with a towel and lie down so it rests on your left side. Do you want me to show you how?

(Oh no, that was not a constructive thought- if I am in her cabin with her and watch her undress, I could not stop myself from urging her to take off the rest.)

He got up and helped her to her feet. "Let's take a walk and see as much of the ship as is possible" He took her arm and put it in his. Since he had grown up in the country, he was not used to walking that way with a woman and he liked the way it made him feel- confident and well mannered.

In fact, he was on the way to becoming a polished lover-Derbyshire's version of Anthony to it's Cleopatra.

Chapter Twenty Six

The next two days at sea were disastrous! A storm came up with huge waves and it was strong enough to separate the seasoned travelers from the novices.

The Tremblant twins, Nettie, Anton, Philippe, Georgie and the cook were overcome. Lizzy still felt ill with morning sickness and could not feel much worse. They thanked God they had Alex along, He was checking for fevers and passed out salt wafers and Kitty followed, enjoying herself in her new role as nurse.

"Do you not understand, Georgie?" asked Alex, "If you had not eaten so many pastries last night at dinnertime, you would be up and around like Kitty. Take my orders on this trip. I do not give them idley, I am the ship's doctor and I am just doing my job."

(Readers, did you notice a drastic change in Alex's medical attitude?- Much too cold and businesslike.)

Georgie hardly recognized the changed man who spoke to her so sweetly the day before.

"Too many pastries! What was he doing, watching me eat through a telescope? His insulting jab made her very angry and that took care of her sea sickness. She was out soon on the deck feeling the boat pitch and turn and getting her sea legs.

"This Savannah must be a devinely beautiful city for any one to go through this more than once," she thought, and almost everyone on the ship shared her feelings.

....

The storm tormented the passengers and some of the crew were bent over with nausea as well.

The girls bustled about, carrying wafers and tea and they were followed by Philippe, who had passed over this wonderful chance to gather sympathy by acting seasick. He was so enraptured with Kitty, he wanted to impress her and had been down on his knees to wipe up some floors where the seasick had been sick.

(Don't you agree that this was monumental progress for a former hypochondriac fop?)

Alex was among the stricken. "Ah, Hah!", Georgie thought, "Too many pastries."

The three caregivers had the tact and kindness to overlook a day of poor hygiene and disarray, and Georgie left a tray with Alex, gathered up his stained clothing and murmured encouraging words.

It demanded concentrated balance to walk while the waves tossed the ship, and they laughed merrily as they slid about the corridors, trying to keep tea in cups and wafers on dishes.

Alex felt slightly recovered and pulled himself up the stairs to the main lobby to reclaim his bearings,

He heard laughter in the kitchen and moved to a chair to get a better view.

There were Georgie and Kitty washing and drying dishes and Philippe was busy with a dustpan and broom.

These two delightful Princesses knew how to keep house!

A Truth, coming to him like a thunderbolt, brought a realization that his stubborness had kept from him.

Rich, refined people are not neccessarily lazy, selfish and helpless, and impoverished, hardworking doctors are not always as sensitive and charitable as they might be.

The vicious storm had subsided and the passengers were on their feet again. As they compared symptoms, they learned that when they were ill, they all thought they might die, and some wished they would.

Georgie mentioned to Kitty that she envied the ladies who had a gentleman to walk arm and arm and was tempted to ask Alex for a stroll. He was so changeable though, she did not know from day to day whether he was in a pleasant mood and liked her, or if she was the last person he wanted to see and ignored her.

Alex was at a fever pitch of medical assistance and romantic insecurity and was often curt with the passengers.

Kitty was always happy to advise and claimed expertise from her position as almost Princess- to- be. "Listen, my dearest and most cherished friend, it cannot hurt to ask Alex for a quick stroll, he is not overly busy and all he can say is, "Yes or no."

During the siege of seasickness, the girls had gathered the passengers' soiled clothing and gave them a good scrubbing to pin them on the clothes line.

She had three items to return to Alex and knocked on his door, announcing, "Darcy's Premier Laundry Company."

Alex was still embarrassed about his illness and to see her first after being so sick, made her look to be God's loveliest messenger, with golden curls fluffed around her head like a halo and wearing his favorite dress.

"Come in, sweetness, close the door, please." He wanted her all to himself for a few minutes. He had been lying in bed and thinking how delicious her skin was and pulled her down to sit on his lap. She had a beautiful long neck just waiting to be kissed, and her arms cuddled his shoulders.

His bed was just beside him, but he had some shreds of honor and after he had kissed her every available unclothed spot, he guided her to the door.

"Georgie, darling, you are the best nurse a sick man could have. God bless adorable you. We are almost to Savannah and I would love to stroll arm in arm with you while we see the sights."

Babette and Nanette were in Heaven. The three days of sickness without meals has slimmed them down and they fit into their costumes again and with promises to perform after dinner, they retired to their cabin to rehearse.

Their spectacular home of the past few weeks, "The Windward," had sailed carefully across the Atlantic one more time without a major incident and the crew gazed through the fog with their telescopes to sight the coastline.

There was a shimmering orange ball on the horizon and the captain thought they would have to do some life saving before they docked in Savannah. As the ship approached, they could see a burning galleon surrounded by row boats filled with sailors.

The Windward sent down rope ladders and the men pulled themselves up with looks of relief and gratitude.

Only two elderly sailors remained in the water and Alex and Philippe dove into the sea to help them catch onto the ladders to reach the deck.

There were twenty eight more passengers and not one spoke English. Babette and Nanette knew Spanish and Italian as well as French and they did some listening and translating. They seemed timid at first, but became proud and sure of their services and they could see that the swarthy group were giving them admiring glances.

The captain told them they were transporting cotton and rice from the Georgia low lands and were horrified at the. thought that all their things would go down with the ship.

"Things!", said the captain of the Windward, "I am familiar with pirate ships and their "Things" are probably gold and silver jewelry they plundered in Savannah. They can not leave the ship soon enough for me."

Nettie knew they were not sailors, they were trying to fool them by removing their large hooped earrings and stuffing the bandanas, they usually wore on their heads to resist the sun, into their pockets. The sailors on the Windward did not wear satin sashes with pockets for daggers and these "sailors" had high leather boots instead of the soft shoes their group wore to save the decks from scratches. They were, at best, sinister, and did not seem like regular folks sailing the high seas, they appeared to Nettie, just like the pirates pictured in story books, and they could not leave fast enough for her, either.

In conversation with the twins, they were vague about their business and solid history and were so tired they fell asleep on the rugs in the main room.

The captain spoke to Alex and William and told them he was sure they could be dangerous after they rested and ate a meal and the ladies on board were wearing wonderful displays of jewels that must be hidden...He was terribly nervous about the women and wanted them in their staterooms.

Philippe could not believe that he had risked his life to save a pirate and the twins would not go along with the captain's orders and proclaimed "The show must go on."

They had good voices and did some astounding dances wearing tap shoes.

160

The Pirate captain could not believe his good fortune. Less than a day ago, he was about to drown in the ocean and today he was watching identical twin sisters doing a dance dressed as a nurse and a Scottish soldier dressed in a kilt.

After the ship landed, the pirate crew set out into the crowd with promises to the Darcys to some day return the favor.

The streets by the dock had sidewalks made of round stones and were terrible for walking. (Especially if one was wearing thin soled satin shoes.) Each of the ladies was carried to the colonel's carriage, and were thrilled to be, back on firm ground again and have some scenery to see.

It was a short ride to the Colonel's mansion by the river and they were driven past neatly laid out squares with fountains and statues brushed gently by blossoms.

Chapter Twenty Seven

Alex looked gloomy. He hated the idea of receiving the Colonel's hospitality and seeing the mansion Georgie would live in if she became his wife.

Lizzy exclaimed that the town was so gorgeous, she had almost forgotten the dreadful voyage and when they were greeted by the Colonel and his sister, Irene, she knew it would be a perfect vacation.

Savannah and it's surrounding land, has large trees supporting lacey moss, and the scene is romantic, and a bit spooky.

All about town, there are gardens of burgeoning bushes of azaeleas. It is a Spanish looking town-just thrilling in a magical way, creating scenes of pastel beauty from the river to far inland.

Alex put his arm around Georgie and whispered "I'11 wager that eight of the trunks are yours." He intended it as gentle teasing, but she was in one of her "prospective missionary wife" attitudes and she pushed his arm away and snapped, "Stop it, Alex, I am not in the mood for your lame humor!"

The day before, when the pirates were lined up facing them at breakfast, he came behind her and asked, "Do we have some Suitable Suitors across the table?"

She socked his arm and said she hoped it would turn black and blue. He watched it blissfully as it did.

"How can anyone be so irritating?" "The prospect of becoming the Colonel's wife in this breathtaking city became increasingly attractive.

Alex had a bedroom with an arousing and decadent display of mirrors on the ceiling. He could see himself in bed with Georgie and Kitty and even Nettie, lounging on pillows placed around him. If you are daydreaming, you may as well go all the way.

The girls were experiencing similar reactions and the maid said that all the bedrooms had mirrored ceilings. What a Den of Depravity.

Kitty and Georgie were not sophisticated by Savannah standards but they were begining to see that they would return as worldly travelers. Philippe was in love with his ceiling but he thought he would warn the rest of their group as a sort of service.

The Colonel had a sister living at the mansion with her small children while their father was at sea with the Navy and each morning their nanny took them for a walk through the squares. She invited Georgie to come along and get her bearings in the city.

All of the other women had men to stroll with and Georgie was feeling a keen sense of loneliness-with Kitty away with her Prince and the twins off beside themselves. They never had to find some one to take on a walk.

When they returned from the lecture tour of Savannah, Alex, who could barely stand to look her way at breakfast, was all smiles and wearing a tattered outfit and asked her if she fished because he was going to Skidaway Island to try his luck and wanted her along. They would take a carriage and buy their poles and lures on the shore.

Georgie loved his invitation because she would have a perfect chance to show him that she reveled in simple pleasure. "I'll be waiting here while you change your clothes." She was wearing a pink silk morning gown and she could not begin to know how to dress for a fishing trip.

The upstairs maid, who was having fun watching these tourists, took her to the attic and opened a dusty trunk. She found some pants and a shirt with a musty scent clinging to them and. even a pair of boots that fit! Because of a burning sun, a certainty in the low lands, a large straw hat was a must and and they found one for Alex too. He would look like a plantation owner.

She looked at herself in a mirror and was reminded of the kidnap.

"Georgie! What is taking you so long?" Alex shouted from the front door. When he caught sight of her, she looked like a short boy, but, never the less, the idea of being in a boat alone with Georgie Darcy was Heavenly. Upon their continuing acquaintance, (It might be called a mishandled love affair) he discovered, with delight, she was a "try anything once" kind of a person and she belonged in the wild somewhere and not shut up in Pemberley. His defense of thinking of her as only a spoiled rich girl, was slowly being chipped away. He stared at her whenever she wasn't looking and was almost

164

startled by her beauty and, almost as important, she was smart and spunky and mischievous. She was so much fun.

His opponents' for her hand in marriage could be limitless and he pictured lines of eligible men leading to her door. He knew he was sometimes moody and difficult but that was caused by the torn up feeling he had in his heart whenever he realized he could never have her... she was actively stating in notes she would never marry him. What a mess! He would wager even a gypsy fortune teller could not lead them out of their confused relationship

"Oh, well, having her as a friend had it's merits too. Three hours of fishing with her!" He taught her how to use the bait and lure from her line and warned that they should whisper. Fishing was a quiet sport. Despite his warnings, Alex paid no attention to his pole and and, instead, told her the story of his life. He was hungry for her to know him and like him. (Readers, it looks to me as if Georgie is in love with Alex and has given him many clues but he is so confused by his new emotions, it is impossible for him to classify the stream of information.) "I think it is your turn now, sweetness, there is no one I would rather listen to than you."

Georgie's story was full of losses. She knew of almost no-one else who had parents who died young and she was not allowed a suitor when William said George Wickham just wanted her fortune.

Through the years of knowing him, they had a gentle love. They played together as children and he taught her to ride and swim. He was a delightful young man and she was charmed by him but William said he was a fortune hunter and sent him away. That was that.

She thought of herself as an unmarriagable heiress from whom everyone stood apart and said, "You have the same notion about me.

People are so surprised when I do things like iron clothes and clean up the kitchen and darn socks for the soldiers. I can even put together a delicious meal. Mrs. Reynolds taught me to cook. I could be a good wife but no one wants to give me the opportunity. Kitty and I laugh all the time about Lizzy searching for "Suitable Suitors," for us. But lately, I do not find it amusing.

I think William really does not want me to marry and move away from Pemberley. He acts as if he thinks no one is good enough for me. I shall be godmother to half the babies in southern England, never having some of my own."

Her eyes began to brim over with tears and Alex stood up and sat beside her to pull her to his chest. He was sad about her history but was having a sublime time just holding and rocking her.

It is never a good idea to rock in a boat. In fact, these two were acting simply childish and, as could be expected, the boat overturned and they were soon hanging on it. Alex looked around, he had been oblivious to all life on earth a few minutes ago, and was relieved to see some "rescuers" smiling broadly and heading out to save them.

Georgie looked beautiful even dressed like a ragamuffin with wet tangled hair. She did not act scared at all and she welcomed another good chance to show Alex what a strong and good sport she was.

"This girl is a living angel," Alex thought, "I have to get on the footing of a respectable engagement. She is right for me, she does not need money, she works hard when she has to, she is not pretentious, she is sweet and loving and smart and we desire each other."

They lay on the beach in the sun waiting for their clothes to dry and he told her he had a dream to see Niagara Falls and expected this would be his only time in America so he planned to take another sea voyage up the coast and then, rides in coaches to the Falls. They had many hotels in the region, so it would not be overly strenuous. He had seen a drawing in a school book and vowed to see them someday.

Georgie had not even heard of Niagara Falls and now she was feeling jealous. She was going to spend some time with Irene at the hospital. Irene kept an hour every day when she went around entertaining the patients playing her flute and when Georgie told her she was a pianist, Irene was pleased and asked her to come along to the hospital parlor, and they practised some duets.

Alex asked if there was a place she would like to see together in Savannah and she came up with a good idea so quickly, he was amazed. There was an ancient cemetery near the squares and she loved the idea of seeing it in the dark. They could bring candles and prepare for a long night. Alex reminded her of the fun they had when they searched for Abigail's stone. She laughed and told him she wanted to write down the engravings on some tombstones. "I love to study history this way, right on the scene. We can take the two seater carriage and tell no one where we are headed, Oh, I feel shivers! I dream of being a novelist, someday I shall write a story about this. It shall be-good" local color" for my novels."

"Anything, little honey, I would like that too."

There were no ghastly shrieks or moans and they could study the engraving on the stones quite easily by the full moon. Alex held a notebook and Georgie told him bits of information to write down. It was not "A Dark and Stormy Night" as is written in many ghost stories, it was a clear and very still night.

They were sitting on the mound of a grave to look at it's stone angel and Georgie felt a breeze on her neck, as if someone was blowing on it. She did not want to scare Alex, but the breeze was following her around the cemetery and she finally could not hold it in.

"Alex, do you feel something blowing on you?"

"Yes, I have been noticing it for about half an hour but I did not tell you for fear you would be scared and I have been having such a good time."

"That is sensitive and generous of you. I like it when you act like that."

Women often leave it to men to make important decisions and Alex was dumbfouded. He did not feel they were in danger, this ghost was a somewhat passive one, although he had heard some ghosts threw things, like severed heads.

"I think we should start by listening, how is that? I grew up with the Pemberley ghost and I was used to his moaning and yelling. He was like a member of the family, let us just walk inside the cemetery as if we do not sense his presence."

("I am with a young woman who is not disturbed by ghosts. I think I had better not act frightened.")

There was a strange predominance of young men killed in duels battling for the hands of lovely maidens. All the stones had explanations of the deaths and this was their favorite, - "Etienne

Pallise, struck dead by a bolt of lightning when there was no storm."
(Now, that was Fate at it's cruelist.)

They agreed this was the funniest, - "Seth Morris- a man who
did not look right or left when he crossed the street. Collided with a
carriage.1782"

They brought a small "Graveyard picnic" of muffins and
grapes and Georgie sat on a tall tombstone. When they opened their
basket, it became very windy and Alex sat by a tree for protection.
"Better come over here with me"

Then she was literally blown off the stone and landed right
next to Alex.

"What do we do now?"

"Grab my book, I have the basket, and run like the Devil."

....

That was a good outing and on the way home in the carriage,
they congratulated each other on their poise in the cemetery.

As they became better acquaintd, Alex was amazed at the bold
and risky personality that was covered over by her social graces. She
was not like her brother, who was reticent and strait-laced. Her
interests were not a society girl's, she seemed to yearn for drama and
the bizarre. She would be a decided challenge as a wife.

Alex guided the horse past the homes they were accustomed to
seeing in daylight, covered with flowers, bright in moonlight.

They told the Colonel of their adventure and he laughed and
said, that they had encountered Whirlwind Willie. No one knew
whose ghost he was but he was often mentioned in stories about
Savannah and he liked to lure tourists into the center statue and then
loved to put on his wind show. "The Ghost Seekers of the Southeast"
had one of their conventions in town and Willie co-operated
beautifully with his wind show and rustled up some ghost friends who
did the most creative hauntings at night in the squares area. We have
hundreds of ghosts in Savannah. Some people do not discuss theirs
because they think the whole thing is "déclassé."

The next day the mail brought happy news and the first was about the birth of Mark Fitz William Bingley, "a hungry and lusty boy with fair coloring like his Mama's."

And the second surprise was of the marriage of Calvin Strand and Mathillda Owen. He told Mrs. Reynolds that he was looking for a tall girl with "meat on her bones" who was a good cook. She worked hard on a project to get him out of her kitchen.

She told Tillie to eat alot of cakes and cookies and she would teach her how to cook and bake her most wonderful recipes.

If she followed her instructions carefully, Det. Strand would fall in love with her and build a magnificent mansion and hire many servants and she would have to merely oversee the cooking.

A very nice part of the story is this. With her extra pounds, Tillie's sharp features softened and she became quite pretty.

The detective was in the dining hall with two of his officers, on invitation of the Darcys, and this is the clever scheme Mrs. Reynolds planned. Tillie was to serve the meal and tell the men she was just helping out but had actually cooked everything under Mrs. Reynolds' instructions. She smiled at her subterfuge and told them she no longer wanted to be the upstairs maid and she was all ready to put an ad in the "London Times" for a position as a cook.

Det. Strand was besotted!

The next week, he arrived with an armful of gifts and they were engaged in no time at all. The building of their manor house was completed, and Tillie was interviewing for her staff.

This is such a happy story because Tillie fell in love with her detective and Mrs. Reynolds, as a matchmaker, was up there with the champions.

Chapter Twenty Eight

Alex's eyes sparkled and he whispered, "I have a surprise for you that you will never guess." He did not think that she would follow him around all the next day, laughing and full of questions and she had the whole household questioning too.

Nettie said she was in on it and she would jump in the river before she would tell.

That Saturday evening, a marvelous ball was held at the mansion for the cream of Savannah society and the gowns and the jewels were the finest in the south. Lizzy and William thought they more than rivaled the Perriers' friends'.

Gardenias and white roses were pinned into the pink curtains, made especially for the party and hanging in louvres at the windows. Each tablecloth was a different pastel and the centerpieces were tall silver vases, above the guests' heads, and overflowing with ferns and camelias.

Irene was delighted with all the compliments. She planned her brother's balls and sometimes ran low on decorating ideas and laughed about it with Lizzy. Alex was sitting next to them and Lizzy said, loudly enough for Alex to hear, "Georgie, if perhaps you marry Fitz William, you could help Irene plan the decorations." No one at the table missed that!

Lizzy had thought for a long time that Alex needed a good jab to move him to propose to Georgie.

Georgie could not stop giggling and held her napkin to cover her blushes. Alex looked alarmed and excused himself, returning to ask her to dance! Everyone at the table watched them and then Georgie knew the answer to the secret! He danced! And, he was splendidly dressed in a black moire suit enhanced with a velvet vest and a white shirt with lace at his wrists.

Georgie beamed as they danced and he told her he had been practising with Nettie as a present for her. She put her fingers on the curls of his neck and kissed him and rested her head on his chest. He cuddled her to him as they danced and he realized that was the fine point of ballroom dancing- a legitimate opportunity to hug lady friends and near strangers!

Men were tapping his shoulder to cut in for Georgie and women tapped shoulders to claim HIM for a dance. To Alex's great delight, he found himself loving the ball and the dancing was such an athletic event, he had to grab Georgie to run out to the garden to rest and cool off.

(Do you remember I predicted a big change in Alex? This country doctor of humble birth and the snobbery to feel superior to-the rich, became a gentleman, a polished, dapper and handsome young gentleman.)

He and Georgie were lying down on the lawn in Fitz' garden, a walled in zoological. place where the animals were very tame. The girls had made friends with two fawns who liked to be fed by hand with carrots and tonight there was a family of raccoons with tiny babies, all wearing their natural "masks" and looking ready for a masquerade. Georgie asked Alex to return to the refreshment table and gather rolls and little cakes for them and she made a trip for a bottle of champagne and two glasses.

They toasted every guest and then raced in to join the dancers for a quadrille. The orchestra was thirty men strong, this was a Big Event and Alex loved it. He considered missionary work a must but he would definitely return to Derbyshire each year for the ball season and his future life would be well danced!

Georgie guessed she had finished her work to prove she was not a spoiled rich girl and on that night of the ball, she was very excited.

On one of their runs from the dance floor to the cool garden and lilly pond, Alex said he must have a swim and stripped off everything but his knee length striped underdrawers and helped Georgie undress for a swim in her bodice and pantaloons.

This was a tipsy pair and Alex called out, "I LOVE YOU Georgie Darcy! BE MY WIFE!"

She swam over to hug him tightly. "Yes, I shall be your wife! Let us honeymoon by Niagara Falls."

....

The morning of their engagement announcement, sent the Fitz William family into a wild explosion of wedding planning.

The setting for the ceremony was "Our Lady of the Blessed Lowlands" Catholic Church.

There was a crowd circling outside for just a glimpse of the stunning bride and groom. Georgie's gown was lightly ruffled with white net and gathered on the skirt with fresh roses. Kitty, the honored maid, led Irene's children down the aisle and placed them around the altar in a haze of pastel satin.

This was the kind of wedding that made the ladies sob and cry at it's beauty and sweet promise.

....

Kitty planned happily for her own wedding in Westminster Abbey, the largest church in London, always used for Royal weddings. She was going to be a Princess and it would be perfect for her wedding to Philippe.

On that day, the Bennets, honored parents, stood outside with bags of rice, and with an arm around her shoulder, Mr. Bennet said, "Mrs. Bennet, I must congratulate you. We have seen five daughters married and our family now has a minister, two men of great wealth and property, an Army officer and a Prince.

You are, indeed, the most able matchmaker in Great Britain."

The End

About the Author

Norma Gatje-Smith grew up in New York City and is a nationally known artist. She graduated from Pratt Institute, studied art in Europe and worked as a designer in the Netherlands and Manhattan.

Her favorite pastime is writing and she has authored humorous essays published in The Chicago Tribune and The Palm Beach Post, and has written numerous articles in magazines.

Her passion for writing began when she wrote to her family about her unexpected adventures while traveling alone through Europe as a twenty two year old.

She lives in St. Joseph, Michigan and Palm Beach County Florida with her husband, Norman Smith, a pilot, who has taken her on many excursions to gather inspiration for her entertaining stories.

Printed in the United States
R900600002B/R9006PG24148LVSX00004B/3}

9 781418 426590